"I just found twenty kilos of cocaine in the back of your van."

Dani blinked. Twice. And then asked him to repeat the statement.

"I found ten bags of cocaine in the trunk of your vehicle." Gideon enunciated each word with careful precision. "Actually, Lou did. I'd estimate its street value to be close to a million dollars."

She gave a gasp of surprise. "Your dog found cocaine in our van?" This had to be a joke. "Is he some sort of supersecret agent canine trained to sniff out drugs?"

The muscle flexing along Gideon's jaw and the firm set of his mouth showed that this was no laughing matter.

"He is. And he's got the medals to prove it. It took him less than five minutes to locate the stash of drugs hidden with the Bibles. Ironic, don't you think?"

Her mind scrambled to make sense of this information. She supposed that, if true, it was rather ironic, but at the moment, that was the least of her concern. "Who put them there?"

"I was hoping you could tell me."

Jaycee Bullard hails from Minnesota, where a thirty-degree day in January is reason to break out short-sleeved shirts. In the ten years since graduating with a degree in classical languages, Jaycee has worked as a paralegal, an office manager and a Montessori teacher. An earlier version of *Framed for Christmas* won the 2016 ACFW Genesis award for Romantic Suspense. Check in and say hi on Facebook at Facebook.com/jaycee.bullard.1.

Books by Jaycee Bullard

Love Inspired Suspense

Framed for Christmas

FRAMED FOR CHRISTMAS

JAYCEE BULLARD

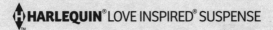

HARLEQUIN® LOVE INSPIRED® SUSPENSE

Recycling programs
for this product may
not exist in your area.

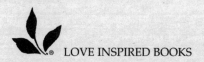 LOVE INSPIRED BOOKS

ISBN-13: 978-1-335-54408-7

Framed for Christmas

www.Harlequin.com

Printed in U.S.A.

To the only wise God our Savior, be glory and majesty, dominion and power, both now and ever. Amen.
–Jude 1:25

Dedicated to my family. Mom and Dad, Nate, Clare, William and Nick. Paul, Jenny, Jen and Mallory. I couldn't have done it without your love and support.

To my friends and colleagues at SPTS—Mark, Jim, Jeff, Courtney, Chris and Kathy—thank you for giving me those Thursday afternoons off to work on my writing. It meant more than you can know.

And to Dina Davis, my editor at Harlequin. I am deeply grateful for all your kindness and support.

ONE

Dani Jones kept her head low as she lifted the nozzle from the fuel tank and set it back on the pump. It was a simple task, but her hands were trembling as she fumbled with the gas cap, trying to screw it on tight. Her eyes flickered toward the tan SUV parked behind her. It was the same vehicle that had been following her since Iowa. Same plates, same driver and passenger, with their ball caps pulled low and their eyes determinedly avoiding contact. She took a deep breath and repeated the familiar words that always steadied her nerves and calmed her racing heart. "I am safe. God is with me. No one is trying to hurt me."

It had been more than fifteen years since her twin sister Ali's brutal murder. Fifteen years without a single incident. She hadn't been mugged, attacked or threatened in any way. But none of that mattered. The anxiety remained.

She inhaled. Exhaled. But she couldn't relax.

The weather had taken a turn for the worse, and the small canopy over the pumps offered little protection from the blowing snow. Squeegee in hand, she set to work swiping through ribbons of sludge on the van's rear window, until a reflection in the glass caused her breath to hitch. The tan SUV behind her was no longer stationary. It was steamrollering forward on a collision course with the back of the van—and her.

Her knees buckled and panic threaded through her senses.

"Stop!" Her strangled cry had no effect. "Hit the brake!" she screamed as she raced to dodge the speeding vehicle. She stumbled onto the raised curb seconds before the SUV slammed into her bumper with a bone-cracking thump, ramming the van forward into the lot.

Indignation trumped fear as she sprinted toward the vehicle, brandishing the dripping squeegee. "Do you know you almost hit me?" she yelled. Her answer came in a spray of pebbles and slush as the driver spun into Reverse and headed toward the exit.

Seconds later, the kids in her mission group tumbled through the service station door. All seven of them in a gaggle of oblivious teenage excitement, sliding along the snow-covered pavement, their voices loud and high-pitched as they raced through the lot and climbed into the van. Their boisterous enthusiasm distracted her from the feelings of unease swirling in her stomach. Why hadn't the driver seen her? Had his brakes failed, or was it something more sinister? Surely the accident hadn't been deliberate. But then, why the rush to flee the scene? She could have been pinned between the vehicles. Crushed. Broken. Dead.

But she couldn't allow herself to think about that now, with the blizzard increasing in intensity and streams of white powder roiling across the road. There was nothing to do but forge ahead. They were less than fifty miles from the nearest town, and more than an hour from their destination. Slow and steady, that was the trick. She just needed to stay alert until they reached the reservation.

She climbed back into the van and signaled her turn onto the highway, her eyes darting in every direction, searching for signs of the tan SUV. So far so good. She tightened her grip on the wheel and directed her focus to the road ahead. An hour passed, and still there were no other cars behind her. According to the GPS, they were five miles from the town of Dagger Lake. Just in time, too. Visibility had decreased to near zero, and thick flakes were blanketing the windshield as quickly as the wipers worked to clear her view. In the rearview mirror, she could see the faces of the kids in the back seat. Two hours ago, they were laughing and singing Christmas carols, but now seven sets of worried eyes watched her every move.

"We're almost there." She tried to sound re-assuring, but she was finding it hard to disguise the anxious tremor in her voice. Dread coiled up within her as a set of headlights flashed in the mirror, closing in fast. "Once we make the turn onto 81, we'll—"

The rest of her sentence hung in the air. A bump shook the chassis, and the van heaved forward, spinning onto a sheet of black ice and careening sideways across the pavement. Frantically, she tried to remember what she had been taught when she learned to drive.

Foot off the accelerator.

Steer in the direction of the slide.

It sounded good in theory, but the tires felt like skis, locked in position and built to glide. Her hands cranked the wheel all the way to the left, but the van was out of control. A second later, the hood tipped off the road, and they were headed down a steep embankment on a slow-motion roller-coaster ride through a pillowy quilt of snow.

She pumped the brakes in a desperate attempt to avoid the tall pine that had appeared out of nowhere directly in their path. The tree loomed larger and larger as the teens in the back seat shrieked in fear. In three seconds flat, her brain went from white-knuckle terror to stunned relief as the brakes finally engaged and the van lurched to a stop just inches from the spiky trunk.

She took a steadying breath and turned to check on the kids.

"Everybody okay?" She craned her neck to peer into the back seat. It was suddenly very dark inside the van as a shower of soft flakes fell from the branches and covered the windows with a frosty mantle of snow.

"We're all fine," Josh, one of the younger boys, reported. "If we had been moving faster, it might have been fun."

Fun?

Stuck in a snowdrift somewhere in North Dakota in the middle of a raging winter storm with no bars on her phone and no way to call for help. *Fun* wouldn't be the word she'd have chosen to describe their predicament.

A sense of dread washed over her as she tried shifting into Reverse, but the vehicle's back wheels only spun deeper into the rut.

"Do you want us to get in front and push?" Josh asked.

It was a tempting thought. But mixing seven excitable teens, a five-thousand-pound conversion van and a thirty-foot tree seemed like a recipe for disaster.

"Maybe we can try it as a last resort." She gave the teenager an encouraging smile as she rechecked the reception on her phone.

There was a sudden movement outside the van as a patch of gray light opened up on the windshield, courtesy of a flat yellow mitten pushing away the snow. Her heartbeat revved as she conjured the faces of the men in the tan SUV. Had they followed the van down into the ditch? A scream caught in her throat as the circle grew wider to reveal the face of a huge hairy stranger with icicles dangling from his beard. White clouds from his breath lingered above his frozen eyebrows, and she stared at him with open-mouthed alarm.

She peered through the windshield, her body frozen with indecision. She needed to think fast while dusk was still a memory in the darkening sky. Pulse racing, she slid sideways on the seat and turned to face the kids. "Sit tight while I check things out." As she pushed the door open and stepped outside, a mini avalanche of snow-flakes fell on her head.

"Are you okay?" the man asked in a voice that was low and husky. "Lou and I were coming through the trees when we saw you take a nosedive into the ditch."

Lou? Who was Lou? She looked past him into the white wilderness but didn't see anyone else. Still, the stranger's concern was heartening. Relief bubbled up in her throat. "Did you notice another car on the road?"

He shook his head. "With the whiteout conditions, the highway was a blur. Why? Was there some sort of problem?"

"I felt a bump right before the accident, and I thought that maybe…" What exactly had she thought? That the tan SUV had pushed the van off the tarmac? Given the slippery road conditions, the idea seemed far-fetched.

"Miss Jones?" Lucy's piping voice trilled from the back seat, pulling Dani's attention to the van. "Are we still going to the reservation?"

"I hope so." Dani turned to once again face the stranger. "Any chance you have a vehicle that can pull us out of here?"

He shook his head. "My truck is out of commission. Even so, it would probably take something with a lot more horsepower to haul a van of this size out of a ditch."

She reached into her pocket and pulled out her cell. "I thought about calling for a tow, but I haven't been able to get any reception. Do you have a landline we could use?"

"Sorry. I don't. I heard on the radio that all of the cell towers are down."

Helplessness washed over her. Something nudged her from the side, and she turned to find a massive German shepherd intent on checking her out. She flinched and took a step closer to the open door. So, this was Lou. The shepherd growled softly and watched her through glowing eyes. Her back stiffened. This probably wasn't a good time to mention her fear of big dogs, especially ones who seemed determined to push their way uninvited into the van.

The man must have sensed her unease, because he looped a mittened hand around the edge of the dog's collar and held him fast. "Lou and I seem to be forgetting our manners. The name's Gideon Marshall, ma'am." He raised his voice to be heard over the gusting wind.

"Nice to meet you, Mr. Marshall. I'm Dani Jones. The kids and I are headed to the Dagger Lake reservation as part of a mission outreach from our local church." She looked up at the dark sky through the thick flakes that seemed to be falling faster by the minute. "But it doesn't look like we're going to make it tonight."

"My cabin is just across the ridge. You're welcome to camp out on my floor until you can arrange for a tow."

Then he smiled, and, despite his huge stature, there was something warm in his crinkling brown eyes that quelled her anxiety.

Lou strained against his master's hold, nudging his large wet nose closer to the van's open door. A stinging gust of wind flicked the end of her scarf across her face and issued a sharp reminder of the dwindling number of options available to her at the moment. She needed to make a decision, and fast.

She stuck her head into the van to address her charges.

"Hey, gang. Mr. Marshall has invited us to crash at his place until we can call for help. Bundle up, grab your gear and get ready to go."

The winds were picking up speed as they climbed up the embankment and began the slow trek to the cabin. Packed-down footholds merged into three-foot-high drifts where the wind had pushed the snow willy-nilly along the path. Dani tried not to overthink her decision to trust the grizzled backwoodsman, but her imagination was running wild, picturing their destination as a run-down shack filled with animal skins and mounted antlers. Or worse.

Gideon strode ahead, undeterred by the blowing and drifting snow. Behind him came a line of stragglers slipping and sliding as they struggled to match his pace. Dani slowed so that she could walk with Lucy, at twelve and a half the youngest of the group. The girl's face was crumpled, and she was on the verge of tears.

"What's going to happen if we don't show up for the opening ceremony at the reservation?" Her voice trembled. "Will someone call our parents and tell them we're missing? What if we get stuck here and don't make it home for Christmas?"

Dani squeezed the young girl's hand through her glove. "No worries, Luce. By tomorrow night, this will all seem like a great adventure."

Or a bad memory. She shivered as a trickle of snow melted into the liner of her thin leather boots. Clearly, she should have chosen more appropriate footwear when packing for this trip, but she hadn't expected to be trekking through a foot of hard-packed snow.

She was panting from exertion by the time they reached the top of the ridge where Gideon stood waiting, his arm stretched out, pointing toward a thick stand of pines. From a distance, the neat little cabin nestled in the center of the grove of trees looked like a scene painted by Thomas Kincaid. To the left of the main building was a barn with a red roof, and set back in the trees, a small garage. Billows of smoke poured out of the cabin's twin chimneys, offering the promise of a warm fire and protection from the storm.

Gideon caught her surprised look and smiled. "I built the place two years ago when I retired. From here it looks small, but inside there's a large open space where you and the kids can bunk for the night."

"You're retired?" Josh sidled up beside them and joined the conversation. "I thought you had to be at least sixty before you did that."

"Most people are," Gideon said. "Not me."

Josh nodded, accepting the answer, but Dani sneaked a surreptitious glance at their host. He walked with the easy gait of someone accustomed to a lot of exercise. She'd guess his age to be late thirties, at the oldest, though it was difficult to tell through his insulating gear.

And then there was the beard. Bristly, untrimmed and peppered with flecks of gray, it looked like a throwback to a different age. But none of the kids seemed bothered by the fact that their host was twice as big as any of them, and three times hairier. They were smiling as they made their way down the ridge, joking about their rescue from the storm. But try as she might, Dani couldn't help feeling just a little bit nervous about entrusting their lives to a stranger, especially one as large and imposing as Gideon Marshall.

Gideon stopped at the bottom of the steep slope and waited for the group to catch up. He hadn't expected the journey to be so slow and arduous. It didn't help that most of the kids were wearing thin canvas sneakers that offered little traction in the deep snow. What had they been thinking when they packed for their trip? It was, after all, mid-December, and a sudden change in the weather was not uncommon for this time of year.

It was hard to blame the kids when their chaperone appeared to be equally unprepared. In her fancy boots and white wool coat, Dani Jones looked like she was heading to a tea party, not a Sioux reservation. Still, he had to give her credit for one thing—he had yet to hear her complain. Lots of people in her position would be grousing about the treacherous conditions, but apparently, she was made of sterner stuff. The expression on her face was kind and sympathetic as she trudged along, offering encouragement to the kids.

Although he had moderated his pace to accommodate the group, Lou showed no such restraint. The high-spirited shepherd leaped from one snowbank to another like a nimble jackrabbit on the chase. At first, Gideon assumed that his dog was just excited to have company along for his walk. But then he began to notice that Lou kept circling back toward the road, his ears perked up on high alert.

The last time he had seen Lou this agitated was during a drug bust on the outskirts of Miami. That had been three years ago, but Gideon could still picture the reactions of the three criminals when the shepherd sniffed out the cache of contraband hidden under the tiles of their kitchen floor.

He hated to say it, but given the way Lou was acting, there was good reason to suspect that there were drugs hidden somewhere in the van. He shot an assessing glance at each of the kids. Three boys and four girls. He wasn't great at estimating ages, but he'd say they all looked to be in their early teens. Sixth or seventh graders, he'd hazard a guess, wholesome and rambunctious with their colorful parkas and expedition backpacks.

Which left Dani Jones. The chaperone. At first glance, she appeared to be a nice enough woman. Pretty, too, with her dark curly hair and bright flashing eyes. But if there was one thing he had learned in his fifteen years on the job at the DEA, it was that appearances could be deceiving. And she sure had acted nervous when Lou tried to put his front paws inside the van. Of course, there was always the chance she was just afraid of dogs, but his gut told him it was more than that. He had seen panic in her eyes when she'd stepped down from the driver's seat, a look of dread that seemed to mask something deeper and more profound. He hoped he wouldn't come to regret inviting the group to his home. Then again, it wasn't as if he had much choice in the matter. He wasn't about to leave them at the bottom of the ravine in the middle of a raging snowstorm.

It was going to be strange to have company after two years of living alone. But being hospitable didn't mean turning a blind eye to signs that something was amiss. Gideon watched as his dog ran in wide circles around the kids, his excitement evident in his every move. Even though Lou couldn't use words to communicate, he knew how to make his thoughts known in other ways. There was a definite set to the shepherd's eyes, a tension in his jaw. And when he started pawing at the ground, as he had been doing when they were back at the van, it was a signal that he was on aggressive alert.

Gideon made a split-second decision as he waited for Dani and the teens to make their way down the incline. As soon as they were settled in for the night, he'd double back to investigate. Even though he no longer worked for the DEA, he still had a responsibility as a citizen. If there were drugs in the cargo hold of the van, he would do his part to stop them from reaching the reservation.

Inside the cabin, he showed the kids where to stow their gear and offered a two-second tour.

"Bathroom, bedroom and open space for all the rest." The kids shuffled into the main room and made a beeline for the floor-to-ceiling windows, which offered a panoramic view of a full moon illuminating the frozen lake.

"Wow!" one of the older boys said as he peered through the glass. "How far is it to the other side?"

"About three miles straight across." Gideon tossed a couple of logs onto the fire and then pointed to a cluster of lights on the other side of the shore. "That's the town over there. Tomorrow morning, if it's clear, you'll be able to see the reservation on the left."

As the kids gathered for a glimpse of Dagger Lake, he rummaged through his cabinets and located a couple of bags of chips. He set them on the counter next to a jug of orange juice and a stack of plastic cups. "Make yourselves at home. I have a few things to do outside, but I'll work on supper as soon as I get back." Five minutes inside a one-bedroom cabin with seven noisy teenagers, and he was more than ready for another walk with Lou in the brisk night air.

The snow was still coming down hard, and a sharp north wind had buried the remnants of their footprints under heavy drifts. Not for the first time, Gideon was thankful for the insulating layers of clothing he was wearing underneath his parka. He had learned early the benefits of trapping his body warmth to keep his core at a comfortable temperature, even when it was below zero.

He'd been five when he experienced his first North Dakota winter, a city boy unaccustomed to the harsh winds and cold temperatures of the northern plains. His father's unexpected passing had left his Sioux mother shattered and bereft, so it fell on her brother, a tribal elder, to take his nephew under his wing. And thirty years later, those early life lessons still remained a part of Gideon's daily routine.

Slipping a high-beam flashlight from his pocket, he flicked it on, even though it didn't look like he was going to need it to help him find his way. The sun had set an hour ago, but the moonshine reflected against a ceiling of light clouds cast a polished brightness on the snow.

In places, the drifts were several feet deep, but he made quick time as he covered the distance between the cabin and the ridge. It was familiar territory. He and Lou hiked this path almost every day. He couldn't recall a time when his loyal shepherd wasn't ready for a walk, and tonight was no exception. Lou might be over-the-hill when compared to his canine colleagues at the DEA, but in many ways, he still seemed like an energetic puppy, always ready to play. But at the moment, Lou stuck close beside him, almost as if he recognized that this particular trek was for work and not pleasure.

As Gideon reached the top of the ridge, he stopped for a moment to enjoy the sharp bite of bitter cold that always made him feel especially alive. This was his favorite time of the year, even though these short days of mid-December held the promise of even chillier weather in the weeks to come. Usually, when he got to this point in his walk, he would hear the gentle hum of traffic on the road ahead. But because of the travel advisory, most people had opted to stay inside for the night. Except... Now, that was odd. A tan SUV with tinted windows and a cracked bumper was parked on the shoulder, its engine idling.

His suspicions clicked to high alert as he approached the vehicle. When he was two feet away, the driver's-side door opened, and a bald man in a navy windbreaker stepped out.

"Hey," the man said. "Quite the night for a walk, eh?"

"It's cold," Gideon agreed as he bent to look at the passenger inside the car. Clean-shaven, stocky build, probably not much of a talker if he were to guess from the man's gloomy countenance. "Do you gentlemen need help?"

"Nope. We're fine." The guy in the navy windbreaker dismissed his concerns with a flick of the wrist. "We're in from Fargo, but we didn't expect this much snow cover on the highway."

"You might want to head home and try back later. The storm's still blowing in, so it'll be rough for a while."

"Thanks," the driver said. "Appreciate the advice." He slid behind the wheel and did a U-turn on the tarmac.

Gideon watched the taillights of the SUV disappear down the road. When it was completely out of sight, he made his way down the embankment toward the van. His eyes fixed on the rear bumper of the disabled vehicle. The V-shaped fold in the center matched the crack he had noticed on the front of the SUV, a fact he filed away for later consideration.

Using a blade from his pocketknife, he pried open the lock on the gate of the trunk. The kids had taken most of their gear when they left for the cabin, but a few random personal items and bits of trash remained. He tossed a notebook and a bag of Twizzlers into the back seat and whistled for Lou. The shepherd jumped into the cargo hold and began sniffing at the floor. Good thing he was trained to ignore food smells. Wrappers and stained paper napkins were scattered everywhere. But Lou was as single-minded as he was tenacious. His nose twitched as he pawed the top of one of the cardboard boxes that had been shoved toward the back of the trunk.

"What's in there, boy?" he asked as he reached over and slid open the flap of a box marked BI-BLES FOR THE RESERVATION. The pleasant scent of new books assailed his nostrils, and for a minute, he entertained the notion that Lou had been mistaken.

He should have known better. Underneath the top layer of Bibles, a dozen or so plastic bags of loose powder formed a soft white nest. His stomach dropped. Even though this was what he'd been expecting, he had hoped for a different outcome. Packets of loose white powder always meant the same thing. Drugs. He fumbled in his pocket and located his phone, which he used to snap a dozen or so pictures of the stash. Good thing he still had a narcotics identification kit at the cabin. He'd test the powder when he got home, but his gut told him it was cocaine. He loaded the packets into his oversize backpack and shoved the box back where he had found it. This wasn't the way they did things back at the DEA, but desperate times called for desperate measures.

At least he was wearing gloves.

His ears still upright, Lou nudged a second box and then a third one. The contents were all the same. Anger surged through Gideon's body like a flame. Even now, two years off the job, the sight of such a huge cache of drugs filled him with revulsion. And fear. There was enough white powder in the back of the van to make someone desperate enough to kill.

TWO

"This place is awesome," Josh exclaimed. "All the furniture is supersized."

"Mr. Marshall has good taste," Mary Kate agreed as she ran her fingers along the cushion of one of the leather sofas in the center of the room. "And look how the gold design of the rug matches the rest of the decor."

"But there's no TV," Gabe pointed out.

"And no Christmas tree, either." Annalise complained. "You'd think with all the pines around here it wouldn't be that hard to chop one down."

"Speaking of trees, did anyone notice the massive pile of wood by the barn?" Josh asked. "It must have taken hours to split all those logs."

"I don't think it was a problem." Joe flexed his biceps in a show of solidarity with their host. "Did you see his arms? He must work out constantly to have muscles that size."

"Let's take a break from the personal analysis

of our host and review the plan." Dani blushed self-consciously as she glanced nervously at the door. She had also noticed Gideon's strong arms, but it would be embarrassing if he walked in and overheard any part of their conversation, especially the comments concerning his physique.

"When do you think we'll get to the reservation?" Lucy asked. "I can't wait to see all the kids we met last summer."

"Soon, I hope." She tried again to get reception on her cell and frowned at the blank screen. "By tomorrow, for sure."

Definitely by tomorrow, if she had anything to say about it. She had been quick to reassure Lucy, but the fact of the matter was that all of their parents would be worried sick when they found out the group hadn't arrived as expected. And, with the phones down, there was no way to let them know that everyone was safe.

"Hey, Miss Jones," Josh called out. "You want a bowl of chips?" He was standing by the kitchen counter, acting like the mayor of Dagger Lake as he dispensed snacks and drinks to the rest of the kids.

"No, thanks," she said. Given the knot in her stomach, it was unlikely she'd have any appetite for dinner. An image flashed through her brain of the expressionless faces of the men at the gas station. Who were they, and why were they following her? She wanted to believe that any sinister thoughts she might conjure were the work of an overactive imagination. But part of her—the part that could never forget what had happened to her sister, Ali—knew that no one was ever safe.

The door banged open and Gideon walked into the cabin, a string of cleaned perch in his hand. "Here's today's main course," he said. "Caught fresh this morning from the best ice fishing hole on the lake."

"I hate fish," Ellie moaned.

"You'll like these," he assured her. "And if you don't, you can close your eyes and pretend you're eating chicken."

Despite the lighthearted banter, there was a marked change in Gideon's demeanor, and Dani wondered what had happened since he left to finish his chores. His mouth was set in an anxious frown, and his eyes were wary. He placed the fish on the counter and turned to face the group.

"Before I start to make dinner, I need to grab a few things from the barn. Maybe your leader can give me a hand. You kids can set the table while we're gone. Paper plates are in the cupboard above the sink, and folding chairs are stacked in the closet by the door."

The edge to his tone made Dani suspect there

was more on the agenda than retrieving supplies. As she slipped on her coat and followed him outside, she found herself wondering what could possibly have happened to explain the shift in his attitude.

She trailed Gideon and Lou along the tramped-down path to the barn, a ramshackle building with a painted red door. Gideon pulled out a set of keys to unlatch the rusty padlock, then opened the door and flicked on a light switch, bathing the space in a shadowy glow. She detected the scent of fresh hay and a slight whiff of something that smelled like oil. In the center of the room was an aluminum boat with a shiny new motor set next to it on a tarp. Along the back wall, an old push lawn mower, some power tools and a few broken chairs shared space with a beat-up snowmobile with a black leather seat held together by duct tape.

Gideon sat on a bale of straw and, with a curt nod, indicated that she should do the same. Lou shot her a look of supreme disillusionment as he curled into a ball beside his master's booted feet.

"I thought we could have a little talk without the kids around." Gideon's face was a mask of shadows in the dim light.

She nodded. She couldn't imagine what he needed to talk to her about, unless he was rethinking his decision to allow the group to stay in the cabin. Maybe he was about to suggest that they set up camp in the barn, which would be fine, though slightly chilly for those whose sleeping bags lacked extra insulation.

But any type of shelter was better than the alternative. She smiled encouragingly, which caused him to glare back at her. He seemed to be expecting a different sort of response, and when he finally spoke, his words could not have been more surprising.

"I just found twenty kilos of cocaine in the back of your van."

She blinked. Twice. And then asked him to repeat the statement.

"I found ten bags of cocaine in the trunk of your vehicle." Gideon enunciated each word with careful precision. "Actually, Lou did. I'd estimate its street value to be close to a million dollars."

She gasped. "Your dog found cocaine in our van?" This had to be a joke. "Is he some sort of super-secret-agent canine trained to sniff out drugs?"

The muscle flexing along Gideon's jaw and the firm set of his mouth showed that this was no laughing matter, even before his words confirmed it.

"He is. And he's got the medals to prove it. It took him less than five minutes to locate the stash of drugs hidden with the Bibles. Ironic, don't you think?"

She scrambled to make sense of this information. After all, she was a scientist who worked with DNA, trained to observe even the smallest detail, but she had neglected to examine any of the boxes before stowing them in the cargo area of the van. She supposed that, if what Gideon said about the drugs was true, it was rather ironic, but at the moment, that was the least of her concerns. "Who put them there?"

"I was hoping you could tell me." His cool, dark eyes lingered on her face as if searching for answers. "I'm at a loss here, trying to figure out what to think about this. You seem like a nice enough lady. And the kids in your group appear to be straightforward and friendly, as well. I'm sure I don't need to tell you that transporting drugs over state lines is a felony. I noticed that your van has Iowa plates, which makes me wonder about your reasons for visiting the reservation. It's hard to imagine why anyone would choose to travel this distance in a raging snowstorm with a bunch of kids who are supposed to be in school."

She bristled at his tone, her dismay giving way to resentment at his innuendo. Who did Gideon Marshall think he was? Yes, he was allowing them to use his home and offering shelter from the storm. And yes, he did look like he could star in his own superhero movie with his broad shoulders and strong arms straining the sleeves of his red flannel shirt. But that didn't give him the right to make those kinds of wild accusations.

"You may find this hard to believe, Mr. Marshall, but I'm just as surprised as you are by all of this. Maybe you should start by explaining what led you to discover these so-called drugs in the first place."

Instead of the look of chagrin she had expected, his lips formed a satisfied smile. "Lou was acting skittish when we came upon you in the ditch, so I decided I needed to check out the situation for myself."

"So you broke into our vehicle and rummaged through our stuff?"

"Exactly." He cocked his head to one side, seeming pleased to admit he had violated their privacy. "And it turned out that Lou was correct, which isn't surprising, since his nose is never wrong. Believe me, Miss Jones, this is not a small amount of contraband we're dealing with. So it would behoove you to answer my question. Why bring a van full of kids from Iowa to North Dakota in the middle of a snowstorm?"

She stared at Gideon Marshall with barely contained irritation. Okay, maybe he knew what he was talking about when he claimed to have found drugs in the van, but they didn't belong to her or anyone in the mission group. She took a deep breath and willed herself to be civil to this man who—she needed to remind herself—had rescued them from an uncertain fate in the North Dakota wilderness.

"We came to Dagger Lake because the new community center on the reservation is opening this weekend. The kids were here this past summer on a mission trip to help out after the flood. As a thank-you, the chief and the council of elders invited them to attend the ribbon-cutting ceremony on Saturday night." She paused to cast a withering glance in his direction. "Apparently, their parents thought the experience was worthwhile enough for them to miss school."

Gideon's lips turned down in a scowl. "Do you have any reason to suspect that anyone in the group might be dealing drugs?"

This was getting more absurd by the moment. "Absolutely not. I can personally vouch for each and every one of these kids." Her voice quavered with anger as she met and held his gaze. "I've known all of them for years, and I can't imagine any of them being involved in something like this. They are all honor students who spend their free time volunteering and doing service projects with our church." An idea occurred to her. "Is it possible that the stuff you found is talcum powder?"

Gideon gave a bitter laugh. "Let me assure you, Miss Jones, that I can tell the difference between talcum powder and cocaine."

"Fine," she huffed. "Let's say for the sake of argument that there really are drugs in the back of the van—"

"Were." He interrupted. "They aren't there anymore. I've secured them in a safe place until I can turn them over to the sheriff." He shot her another hard stare. "I get the feeling you doubt my credentials. Maybe you see me as some sort of crazy backwoodsman who doesn't know the difference between oregano and pot."

She felt the blood drain from her face. "You found pot in the van, as well?"

"I was just using that as an example to make my point," he said, his voice thick with frustration. "Listen. I should have said this right at the outset. I used to work for the DEA, which means that I've had plenty of experience dealing with illegal drugs. This isn't just a hunch. It is fact. I used a testing kit to confirm that the powder is definitely cocaine. So you can see that I'm not making an idle accusation. I know what I'm talking about, and when I tell you someone in your group is guilty of smuggling drugs, you can be assured I don't make the accusation lightly.

Which brings us back to the question—who hid the stash in your van?"

"I have no idea." Her head was spinning as she tried to wrap her brain around what Gideon had just said. Had he just called her a criminal? Maybe not directly, but certainly by inference. And what was a DEA agent doing living in the middle of nowhere? Scratch that. A retired DEA agent. Dani looked again at the man sitting across from her. She wanted to tell herself he was a fraud or, to use his own words, a crazy backwoodsman, but something in her gut told her that, despite his disreputable appearance and intimidating size, Gideon Marshall was telling the truth.

"Let's try it another way. Start with a list of people who had access to your vehicle, and we'll work forward from there."

This would be the moment to tell Gideon about the two men in the tan SUV. And yet, she hesitated. Who knew how he'd react to the news that she had failed to report the incident at the gas station? He already thought that she was irresponsible for driving through the blizzard. Why add fuel to the fire?

"My name would be the only one on that list. I packed the trunk myself last night after the kids dropped their gear off at church. Once everything was loaded, I pulled the van into the garage where it stayed until this morning."

"Where did the boxes with the Bibles come from?" Gideon leaned forward, his chin in his hands and his elbows on his knees.

Was it her imagination, or was this "little talk" turning into a full-scale interrogation? If she and Gideon were actors in a TV crime drama, this would be the moment when she'd refuse to answer any more questions until she talked to her lawyer.

"I don't know." She shrugged. "They were stacked by the pile of gear, and the boxes were marked BIBLES FOR THE RESERVATION."

"No signature?"

She shook her head.

"Didn't that make you suspicious?"

She bit her lip. At the very least, it should have made her curious, but she had been in such a hurry to finish packing that she hadn't given it a second thought. "This was my first time chaperoning, so I just assumed that bringing along Bibles was part of the routine. We are a church group, after all."

Gideon shifted forward. "I noticed the name of your congregation stenciled on the side door of the van. Who's in charge of maintenance for the vehicle?"

"The custodian at the church. But there's no

way he's involved in this. He's been around for as long as I can remember. And he's at least seventy-five, with a bad back, so clearly, he doesn't fit the profile."

"Doesn't fit the profile?" Gideon repeated her words with more than a trace of cynicism. "When you've worked with the DEA for as many years as I did, you learn that just about everyone fits the profile."

Gideon turned up the heat under the frying pan as he prepared to sear the fillets. A shortage of supplies had forced him to keep the menu simple—fresh fish, a green salad, a dozen or so cut-up oranges and a crisped loaf of day-old bread. He was glad he'd made it to the grocery store yesterday before the storm. He just hoped there would be enough food to satisfy a group of hungry teens.

As he added a couple of pats of butter to the pan, he took a moment to consider the likelihood that Dani Jones was not the innocent chaperone she seemed to be and was instead the ringleader of a major drug-smuggling operation.

The jury was still out on that one. In his experience, beautiful women tended to attract trouble, and Dani Jones was definitely beautiful. On their walk back from the barn, he'd noticed how the snowflakes stuck to her long dark lashes and how her cheeks glowed from the cold. He did admire her spunk and loyalty when she rallied to the defense of the kids. A woman like that had courage. And she had seemed genuinely surprised that the Bibles had been used as decoys to hide cocaine. But sincerity could be used to mask duplicity, and very few people were who they pretended to be.

He'd learned that lesson the hard way, first as a child growing up on the reservation, and later at the DEA, when Jonas—his partner, a man he had trusted with his life—set him up to take the fall for the death of an innocent witness. Gideon still found it hard to wrap his head around the facts of the betrayal. A seemingly airtight case against a ruthless drug lord that hinged on the testimony of a brave young woman. It should have been a slam dunk. But, instead, he had let his guard down and allowed Jonas to take the lead on the investigation, unaware of his partner's sinister agenda. Could the same type of subterfuge be true of Dani? What sort of deceit was she hiding behind that guileless face?

Complicating matters was the unlikely coincidence of the tan SUV with the dented bumper idling near the spot where the church van had skidded off the road. Did that prove that Dani was telling the truth, at least in her suspicions about being knocked off the road? Without more conclusive data, it was impossible to say.

As the group took their seats around the table, he set two heaping platters of fish in the center and then slid into an open chair between two of the kids. But before he could give the call to dig in, the petite blond-haired girl on his left—Lucy, if he remembered correctly from Dani's introductions—reached over and took his hand. He glanced at her to see what she wanted, but her eyes were shut. So were Dani's as she began to pray.

"Lord Jesus, thank You for the warmth of this cabin and for the companionship of good friends. Thank You for keeping us safe and for helping us find shelter from the storm. And thank You for the food You have provided to nourish our bodies and for our host, who rescued us from the ditch and cooked this meal before us on the table. We are grateful for his hospitality and kindness."

Beside him, Gideon's neighbor gave his fingers a quick squeeze before releasing his hand.

He let out a long breath. It was hard enough having his personal space invaded by a small army of excitable teens. But now he was being forced to hold hands and say grace. Talk about being pushed out of his comfort zone.

For over two years, he had been preparing and eating meals at the cabin, and this was the first time he had even thought about thanking God for his food. After what had happened to his family, he wasn't exactly on friendly terms with the Man Upstairs, so it wasn't all that surprising.

Still, the kids and their chaperone seemed to take comfort in spending time in fellowship and prayer. Maybe he could take advantage of their relaxed mood to do a little digging into the circumstances of their visit to Dagger Lake.

"Miss Jones tells me that your youth group is based out of Mason City. Go, Hawkeyes, right?"

"We're from Blooming Prairie, actually," Josh corrected. "And most of us prefer the Cardinals."

Gideon raised an amused brow. "Good to know. And were all of you part of the original group who visited the reservation this past summer?"

"Yup." Josh seemed comfortable assuming the role of spokesman. "Only, Mr. Anderson was our chaperone the first time we came."

"Mr. Anderson, huh? What's he like?"

At the far end of the table, Joe grinned. "He's okay. He's the choir director at our church, and he's really big into Gregorian chants. We actually prefer Miss Jones."

Gideon nodded. It wasn't hard to see why. Before sitting down to dinner, Dani had pulled her hair back in a braid, and her clear gray eyes seemed to sparkle every time she turned to face the kids. With her calm demeanor and sympathetic smile, she clearly was one of those people who related well to teenagers. He would definitely have been one of the boys crushing on her when he was their age. Unfortunately, that was then and this was now. At the moment, she was his number one suspect in a drug-smuggling case. "What kinds of things did you do at the reservation?"

"A little bit of everything," Josh answered again. The kid acted like he was thirteen going on thirty. "Babysitting. Playing basketball with the younger kids. A few of us lent a hand helping restore one of the murals that was damaged in the flood."

Gideon settled back in his chair and listened to the kids talk about the jobs they had done on their first visit to Dagger Lake. Many of the homes on the reservation had been ravaged by the high waters of the early-spring floods, and it was difficult not to admire the group's willingness to travel such a distance to help out. The kids were direct in answering his questions, but their leader was acting skittish. In the last five minutes, Dani Jones had spilled a glass of water, knocked over a saltshaker and twice dropped her napkin onto the floor. He was starting to think there was something about him that made her nervous.

He must have been staring again, because she gave him an inscrutable look when she met his eye.

"This is a lovely cabin, Gideon." *Gid-ee-yun.* She drew out the syllables of his first name, making it sound foreign and exotic. "How long did you say you've been living here?"

"Two years," he replied. He was amused to see she was doing a little interrogating of her own. "But I've owned the land for quite some time. I used to keep a trailer on the property for fishing in the winter."

"Cool," Joe exclaimed. "I still can't believe you can catch perch through a hole in the ice."

"It's pretty easy, actually. I use a hand auger to cut a seven-inch circle, and then all I need to do is drop in my line and see what I can pull up. The ice is already pretty thick this year. Some of the guys in town haul out their shacks in early December, but I usually wait until January."

He noticed that Dani was frowning as she peered across the room. Apparently, she didn't find his description of ice fishing all that scintillating.

"Is everything all right?" he asked.

Dani nodded. Something was bothering her, but if she didn't want to tell him, he wasn't going to pry it out of her. And before the group got too comfortable, he needed to review the plan for the evening and next day.

"Why don't we take a moment to discuss the sleeping arrangements for tonight? Gentlemen, how about we let the ladies have the bedroom, and we'll set up on the living room floor?" When no one protested, he continued. "Tomorrow morning, I'll do my best to get you to the reservation. Unless you'd prefer to stay here indefinitely to hang out with Lou and me." He forced a wry grin to show that he was joking. "I'd like to get an early start, so all of you need to be prepared for a 7:00 a.m. departure."

A couple of the kids groaned.

"Are we going to walk across the lake?" Lucy asked.

He shook his head. For the second time that evening, he kicked himself for not ordering the parts to fix his truck. "The drifts are too deep for that. I'm going to take you by snowmobile, but I can only fit one at a time."

"Fun!" Gabe exclaimed.

"That might be an overstatement, but it shouldn't be too bad. I have extra gear to help you stay warm. Like I said before, it's a pretty straight shot from my dock to the sheriff's office on the other side. When we get there, you can call your parents and let them know you're okay. Sheriff Stanek may want to ask you a few questions, but after that, he'll arrange to get you to the reservation in time for the ceremony."

"Questions about what?" Josh homed in on the million-dollar detail.

Gideon stood and walked over to the stove to pour himself a cup of hot water from the kettle, taking his time to stir in a tablespoon of coffee granules before rejoining the group. The kids were young, but that didn't mean that they shouldn't know the truth. Besides, they were going to find out soon enough. "Earlier this evening, I discovered a significant quantity of cocaine in the back of your van. I discussed the situation with Miss Jones, and she was quick to assure me that no one in your group is involved with either taking or smuggling drugs. So, unless someone wants to make a confession, I'm going to operate on that assumption, but only temporarily. If you don't mind, I'd like to ask you a few questions about your preparations for the trip. Are you all okay with that?"

Seven heads nodded in unison. Their solemn faces reflected the seriousness of his request.

"Good. Let's start at the beginning, then. Miss Jones has already explained most of the details of your mission trip. But as you think about the days leading up to your departure, I'd like you to try to remember if you noticed anything out of the ordinary that caught your attention. Maybe it was something as simple as spotting someone carrying a box through the parking lot when you arrived with your gear. Or maybe it was a person you didn't know very well who was asking too many questions about your plans. Basically, I'm interested in anything and everything you might have seen or heard that relates to your visit to the reservation."

There was a long silence. Josh and Gabe shifted uncomfortably in their seats.

"Gentlemen?" Gideon asked. "Do you have something to add to the discussion?"

Josh suddenly looked a lot less confident as he turned to meet Gideon's eyes. "I... We...don't really know if this is the kind of thing you're looking for, but after Gabe and I left our stuff at the church, we thought we saw a car that looked like my mom's at the far end of the lot. The driver was slumped down, talking on his phone. When he saw us approaching, he reached across to the passenger seat, picked up a gun and held it in front of the window." Josh gave a nervous laugh. "We took off running and didn't look back. At least I didn't," he added with a shrug.

Dani gasped. "A gun? Boys! Did you tell Josh's mom?"

Josh looked at Gabe, who shrugged sheepishly.

"We thought that if we said something, our

parents might not let us go on the trip," Gabe explained. "And when we talked about it later, we decided it was probably a toy and the guy was just trying to scare us so we'd leave him alone."

"Did you happen to notice the plates on the vehicle?" Gideon wanted to know.

"No," Josh admitted. "But it was a white Jeep."

A white Jeep, not a tan SUV. Interesting. "And you didn't recognize the driver?"

Josh's laugh was high-pitched. "No. He was wearing a hoodie, so I didn't get a good look at his face."

"How about the rest of you?" Gideon asked. "Did anyone else see or hear anything unusual?" His eyes made a loop of the circle, finally coming to rest on Dani. There was something nervous and wary in her eyes. It was a look he had seen often during his years at the DEA, although it was usually the victims, not the perpetrators, who wore that expression of panicked confusion. It was as if there was something she wanted to share but didn't know quite how to bring it up. "Dani? Is everything okay?"

Dani's fingers trembled as she raised them to her lips. "I just saw a shadow of something moving outside."

Gideon pushed back his chair and walked over to the large picture window. "It's probably a deer looking for food. I'm surprised Lou's so quiet. He usually sounds the alarm when anyone gets close to the house."

On cue, the dog perked his ears and began to bark.

"Like I said, there's a good chance that it's just a hungry animal, but it can't hurt to check things out." He slipped on his coat, grabbed a flashlight from the shelf and pointed at Lou. The shepherd jumped up. Clearly, he didn't need to be asked twice.

For a moment, no one spoke. Then Joe stood and folded his arms across his chest.

"I'll bet it's a bobcat," he said. "Don't worry, Miss Jones. Lou will scare it away."

"Or maybe it's a moose," Gabe suggested. "Or a mountain lion?"

"Or a gray wolf or a coyote?" Josh almost spilled his glass of juice in his excitement. "Maybe we men should help Mr. Marshall look for tracks."

Gideon shook his head. "Thanks for the offer, boys, but it might be best if you stay back and help with the chores." Given the fact that the drugs were now hidden in his barn, he couldn't discount the likelihood of a far deadlier threat.

THREE

Gideon stood at the top of the ridge and surveyed the landscape. The snow was still falling in large wet flakes, thickening the shape of the trees and bushes, bending their limbs and making them unrecognizable. Most nights this time of year, he'd be in his cabin, restringing his favorite fishing pole and enjoying the solitude. Over the past two years, he had grown accustomed to his own company, keeping his own hours, setting his own pace. He suppressed a weary sigh and recommenced his trek. He would make one full circle of the property, and if he didn't notice anything suspicious, he'd return inside. No sense in remaining out in the cold any longer than necessary.

Most likely the shadow Dani had seen in the window was just an animal venturing out of the hills to scavenge for food. He had heard a couple of folks in town mention that at least one bobcat had been spotted along Highway 12. The early snows of October and November had never melted, making it difficult for the larger animals to prepare their winter stores. Still, most were smart enough not to venture out in this kind of storm. With temperatures dropping below zero, they'd more likely be searching for a dry space to lie low and wait out the blizzard. But Lou's tensed back and quivering nose confirmed that something or someone was definitely on the prowl nearby.

A gale of wind buffeted the cluster of sumac next to the road. A ribbon of color on one of the branches caught the beam of his flashlight. Stuck on a twig was a scrap of blue cloth that hadn't been there that morning. Gideon's neck muscles coiled as he examined the fabric. Hadn't one of the men he'd seen earlier in the tan SUV been wearing a parka of a similar color?

Which brought him back to the drugs in the van and Dani Jones. Her nervous mannerisms contradicted her assertion of innocence, but he didn't get a guilty read on her, either. She was hiding something, but whether or not it involved the smuggled drugs, he didn't know. Her story warranted closer examination.

But not by him.

No, he wasn't about to break any of the promises he'd made to himself two years ago when he left Miami. His instincts had failed him once, but never again. He was done being a hero. He was done believing in a greater good.

But Dani was reinvigorating his long-dormant inclinations of chivalry and valor. Despite what he might tell himself, deep down he recognized that he wanted to be the one to save her from whatever trouble she was in.

And he resented those feelings with a vengeance.

He had vowed to never again let down his guard and trust. Not that it was a great hardship. He had always been a loner. That was the way he liked it. Years of being a misfit growing up on the reservation, belonging to neither the tribe nor the town, had toughened his spirit and taught him to enjoy his own company.

Even at the DEA, he hadn't fitted in with the other new agents, with their eager enthusiasm and zealous ambition to make the world a safer place. He had been recruited for his brawn and ability to think on his feet. And he had loved the thrill of the job. An added bonus was having a partner who became his best friend. Jonas had pulled him into his large, extended family, refusing to accept his usual excuses for wanting to be alone.

And after fifteen years on the job, Gideon knew that he was good. One of the best. Which made what happened two years ago all the worse. He could still see the crushed look on the old lady's face when he told her that her daughter wasn't coming home. That, despite his promise to protect the witness, he had failed in his mission and a young woman was dead.

The nightmare lasted for several months, and by the time Internal Affairs produced their report, he was a different man. Cynical and distrusting. It didn't matter that the DEA offered to reinstate him as an agent. He was soured on the job and angry at the world. His friends and fellow agents had turned on him, and he had become an outcast, a victim of the very system that he had worked so hard to maintain. A week after his partner was arrested for the murder of Maria Guterez, Gideon returned home to North Dakota, a place he had vowed to never return.

But the harsh and desolate landscape had proved to be good for his soul. And the lessons he had learned as an agent were ones he never forgot. Even now, as he reached the top of the ridge, his senses shifted into high alert. Above the din of the howling wind and creaking trees, there was the unmistakable hum of an engine. He directed his flashlight toward the road twenty feet away and bobbed the beam to the left and right. *There! In the distance! The outline of an SUV!* He couldn't discern make or model, but it could very well be the same vehicle he had spotted earlier.

Of course, everyone in North Dakota drove a pickup truck or SUV. But few were foolish enough to waste time and gas idling on a deserted road, especially in a blizzard. There was only one plausible reason to explain why the two men had returned in the middle of the storm. They had some connection to the drugs. And if that was the case, they were probably armed and dangerous.

He flicked off his flashlight and waited for his eyes to adjust to the darkness. It was unclear if the men were still in their car, but given Lou's heightened tension, it was likely that at least one of them was prowling in the area. Without a weapon of his own, approaching the vehicle would be a foolish course of action, and, with eight civilians under his roof, he needed to beat a hasty retreat.

Pivoting on his heel, Gideon whistled for Lou.

They needed to make it back to the cabin before the men made their move. With twenty kilos of cocaine at stake, they would be desperate to recover the contraband, though he doubted they'd think to look for it in the barn under six inches of hay. Even so, it gave him a sense of relief to know that the cabin itself was secure. The windows had been constructed with tempered glass, and locks and dead bolts fortified the extra thick front and back doors.

As for Dani's role in the operation, he wasn't about to speculate. She could well be the innocent bystander she claimed to be. Or she might be the third partner, gone rogue. It didn't matter. It would be the sheriff's job to sort it all out.

He picked up his pace, adrenaline and anxiety powering his muscles. It was fortunate that he was familiar with the terrain. Without the flashlight, the only trail markers were formless shapes hidden under a blanket of snow. Dampness had not yet permeated his insulating coat and boots, but crystals of ice clung to his beard. Finally, up ahead, he saw the lights of the cabin and the familiar outline of its sloped roof. He trained his eyes forward and faltered.

Just outside the doorway, illuminated by lamp light, stood Dani Jones. A section of dark, curly hair had come loose from her braid and framed her delicate features. His heart tightened in his chest and an unfamiliar longing for love and companionship flooded his senses, but, as quickly as the emotions formed, he tamped them down. What was she doing outside the cabin, anyway? The sight of her peering into the darkness was certainly suspicious. It almost seemed like she was trying to signal someone.

He squatted down, rocked back onto his

haunches and narrowed his eyes, ignoring the bitter cynicism swamping his soul. If Dani was planning a rendezvous, he intended to catch her in the act. With her hand pressed to her forehead, shielding her eyes from the falling snow, she was definitely looking for someone. Him? Or the men in the SUV?

As she took another step away from the doorway, Lou sprang forward with a muffled growl.

And then Gideon heard it, too.

The telltale click of a shotgun pump.

Pulse pounding, he could hardly hear his voice as he bellowed out in the darkness. "Get down!" But Dani didn't seem to hear him. She stood frozen on the threshold, her eyes staring straight ahead.

A howling wind stung her face, and dampness soaked through her sweatshirt and into her bones. Shivering, she wrapped her arms around her waist and took another step out the door, wishing she had told Gideon about the incident at the gas station. But, in her desire to protect the teens, she had hesitated. Her own experience had taught her how easily terror could build upon terror. But now she didn't want to waste another minute. She needed to tell Gideon about the men in the tan SUV. She couldn't explain why. She just knew that she had to do so right away.

She never questioned these rare moments of intuitive clarity. On only two other occasions had she ever felt this kind of deep stirring in her soul. The most recent time had been four years ago, when her pastor had been seeking volunteers to help with the youth ministry at her church. His appeal had struck an immediate chord, and directly after the service, she had signed up. The other time was fifteen years ago, when she had taken off running, sprinting across the field with all her might, her twin sister Ali's voice urging to her to go faster.

But she would have to wait until Gideon returned. The snow was falling too fast and thick, and if she ventured much farther from the cabin's front door, she might get lost in the enveloping darkness.

"Miss Jones?"

A hand reached out and touched her arm. She turned to see Joe at her side, claiming her attention with worried eyes.

"Lucy is crying because Josh said we won't be home for Christmas, even though it's still more than a week away." Joe's brow furrowed in a quizzical expression. "But he's wrong, right? Mr. Marshall said he'd take us across the lake tomorrow."

Dani swallowed her rising frustration. It was hard to blame the kids for being querulous. They had already spent over eight hours trapped in a van, and now they were stuck at a stranger's home, waiting out a blizzard.

She turned and smiled down at Joe.

"Josh is just kidding around. You heard what Mr. Marshall said about…" Her voice caught in her throat as a loud pop ricocheted through the cold night air.

Her feet stumbled beneath her as she grabbed Joe's arm and pushed him inside. She didn't know what the sound they had heard was, but it couldn't be good. Slamming the door behind them, she turned and looked into seven terrified sets of eyes.

"What was that noise?" Annalise asked.

"I don't know. But just to be safe, why doesn't everyone get away from the windows and sit on the floor behind the couches?" Dani sank onto her knees and put her arms around Lucy and Mary Kate, who were sniffling back tears.

"It sounded like a gunshot," Josh said.

Yes, it did, but she needed to stay calm. "There are lots of things that could have made that noise."

"Like what?" Josh wanted to know.

"A tree falling. A branch breaking." Her mind scrambled to come up with other plausible explanations. "A car backfiring. Someone setting off a flare. And even if it was a gunshot, remember, we're in the country. It's possible that someone is hunting."

Lucy edged a little closer. "Or maybe it has something to do with the drugs that Mr. Marshall found in the van."

She had been thinking the same thing.

Tears streamed down Lucy's cheeks as she clutched Annalise's arm. On Dani's other side, Mary Kate and Ellie huddled next to a sea of pillows. Josh and Joe opted for a tough guy look with their arms crossed and their eyes on the door, while Gabe appeared to be praying. Either that or he was deep in thought. She could imagine how she would have reacted when she was their age. No doubt, she would have been holding her sister Ali's hand, looking worried and scared, while Ali, tough and brave, would have sat tall, her back straight, prepared for action.

She shook her head to dislodge the image. Now was not the time for thoughts of what could have been. Despite the reassurances she had offered the kids, she was reasonably certain that the sound they had heard was gunfire. Maybe it was true that someone was hunting, but a winter blizzard hardly seemed like the time for that. Back home in Iowa, there were always a few brave souls grocery shopping or even working out during torrential rainstorms and tornado watches. Somehow, she didn't think it was quite the same thing, but the possibility brought some comfort.

The cabin door slammed open, and two of the girls screamed as Gideon stepped across the threshold. Gone was the kindness that had earlier filled his eyes. In its place was the steely glint of determination. "Is everyone okay?" he asked.

Dani nodded, smoothing her face into an expression that she hoped masked her anxiety.

Gideon gave a curt nod before he disappeared into the bedroom, only to return a moment later carrying something in his arms.

"Is that a crossbow?" Joe's voice was tinged with excitement. "I've only ever seen those in video games and in *Star Wars*."

With another curt nod, Gideon pulled a chair across the room and set it facing the door.

The three boys crowded around for a better look.

Dani found her voice at last. "Was that a gunshot we heard?" With each minute that ticked by, she could feel tension tightening her body and turning her stomach into knots.

"It was." Gideon's tone was calm and collected. But in his eyes was a guardedness that she recognized all too well. It was the same expression she saw staring back at her in the mirror every night as she prepared for bed. "But the situation is under control."

What did that mean? Nothing was under control. Gideon was obviously worried. His finger hovered near the trigger of the crossbow, and his eyes remained fixed on the door.

Josh reached out and touched the polished wood of the bow. "Can I help guard the cabin?"

"Me, too." Gabe and Joe clamored in chorus.

Dani sat back and took a deep breath, willing herself not to panic. The kids appeared to have complete faith in the adults in charge. Listening to the murmur of conversations around her, she felt her angst uncoil. She was reminded again of why she loved working with young teens. They still had such an innocence and enthusiasm about the world around them. In a few years, they might become blasé and tuned in to their cell phones. But for the moment, they were still full of trust and acceptance.

"Why do you have a crossbow? Don't you own a gun?" Gabe wanted to know.

The corners of Gideon's mouth bent into a frown.

"There are a few rules about owning a firearm. Keep it locked up where a child can't reach it. Always leave the safety on and check the chamber before setting it down. Make sure to clean it before putting it away. And there's one more thing that my grandfather taught me. It's that angry people have no place owning guns."

"Are you angry?" Gabe asked.

Gideon nodded his head. "For a long time, I was."

The boys seemed to accept this at face value, but it gave Dani pause. The wariness in Gideon's eyes hinted that there was a story behind that statement, but it wasn't her place to ask. Besides, something more pressing was on her mind. She needed to find a quiet moment to tell Gideon about the men in the SUV. But not with the kids around. She'd wait until after they had gone to bed.

Less immediate concerns distracted her, as well. She made a mental tally of things she needed to do the next day. Notify the parents about the accident, arrange for a tow, think of a way to thank Gideon Marshall for his hospitality. Flowers? Candy? Which would he prefer?

Making lists always calmed her. Her counselor had said it was her coping mechanism in times of stress. As long as she could keep her mind focused on the mundane, she could quell the anxiety churning in her stomach.

She looked up at the clock and was surprised to see that it was after ten. The girls had already excused themselves and headed into the bedroom, but the boys had become more energized by the second as they discussed ways to defend the cabin in the event of an attack.

"What would you say to loading explosives on the head of a sledgehammer, which we could slam into rocks to cause an explosion?" Joe was bouncing with excitement. Dani could only wonder about the safety of such a tactic, but Gideon appeared intrigued, though she suspected he was just humoring the kids.

"What kind of explosives are we talking here?" he asked.

Listening as Joe described the details of the proposed detonation, Dani swallowed her third yawn. She had been waiting for the right moment to tell Gideon about the tan SUV, but she hadn't accounted for three sets of ears listening to their conversation. It would be easy enough to ask him to step into the kitchen, but a whispered exchange could provoke the kind of fear she had been trying to avoid. In any case, it was time to bring the boys' discussion to an end, even if it meant never hearing Joe's other idea about building a catapult and using it to fire logs at the intruders.

"It's time for bed, guys." Dani walked across the room to where Josh and Joe were slumped on opposite ends of the couch. She pointed to the closet. "Grab your gear and get ready for lights-out."

She was grateful Gideon had insisted that the females take the bedroom. Given all of the male bonding that was going on, she would be glad to have a quiet place to retreat.

A bit of grumbling greeted her pronouncement. But ten minutes later, the boys had settled in for the night, and she was stretched out alone on a king-size bed. She had offered to share, but the girls demurred, choosing instead to spread their sleeping bags out on the floor. At the moment, they looked like a litter of newborn puppies, nestled together for warmth.

The headboard of Gideon's bed was made of rough-hewn pine, and she wondered if he had carved it himself. A simple green-and-white quilt was tucked over the pillows, and a couple of extra blankets were folded at the bottom. The mattress was firm and spacious, but she couldn't find a comfortable position to sleep. She curled on her left side, thrashed around and then switched to the right. Settled on her stomach. Flipped to her back. Satisfied at last in her original position, she closed her eyes and said a prayer for strength and fortitude in the days ahead.

Pulling the quilt up tight against her chin, she fell into a restless slumber, her hands clenched in two tight fists. A few hours later, she woke with a start, her heart beating double time in her chest. She had been dreaming of Ali, as she often did in times of stress, and the nightmare lingered, disorienting her senses, before the memory of the day before came flooding back into her mind. The accident. The drugs. The gunshot.

It was impossible to believe that only yesterday evening she'd parked her car in front of the church and headed inside with her checklist for the trip. Coming off an extra crazy day at the lab, she hadn't been able to stop thinking about the pile of paperwork she had left unfinished on her desk.

Distracted as she had been, it was still hard to believe that she was the one who had loaded the drugs into the back of the van. She was usually so meticulous about wanting everything to be arranged just so, but she had hurriedly tossed the cargo into the trunk in order to finish before the custodian locked the doors. As she thought about it now, the boxes had seemed a bit wobbly when she lifted them. But it would have been a huge leap for her to suspect that they contained bags of cocaine. As for the boxes, she could picture the large block letters. BIBLES FOR THE RESERVATION. Maybe she should have questioned the absence of a signature. But she hadn't given it a second thought.

The idea that someone would view a mission

trip to a Sioux reservation as an opportunity to smuggle cocaine hadn't even been on her radar. Her biggest worry had been staying alert for the long drive, so she had started the morning with a jumbo mug of gas station coffee, which she'd refilled twice along the way. Now, as she tossed and turned on the unfamiliar bed, she was paying the price for all of that caffeine.

Suddenly thirsty, she pulled on her sweatshirt and headed to the kitchen for a glass of water. It was a bright night with a full moon illuminating the room in a soft golden glow. She tiptoed past Josh and Gabe, out for the count in the middle of the floor, and Joe, who had won the game of rock/paper/scissors to claim the second couch. She didn't notice Gideon until she was standing at the sink, getting ready to turn on the tap. She had an eerie sense of someone watching her, and when she turned, she saw him sitting on a straight-backed chair by the window, crossbow at the ready and Lou by his side.

"Hi," she whispered, moving quietly across the room to where he was seated. "I was just getting a glass of water. Is everything okay?"

"Yup. Lou seemed jittery, so I thought I'd sit with him a bit."

By the light of the fire, with the stray icicles brushed out of his beard, Gideon looked a bit less foreboding. He ran a hand through his long dark hair, pushing it back from his chocolate-brown eyes. She glanced at Lou, who appeared to be enjoying his master's undivided attention after a long, hard day. He was lolling on his back, his large pink tongue poking lazily out of the side of his mouth as he waited for his belly to be scratched. If dogs could talk, he would probably tell her to go away.

"Do you think the man with the gun is still out there?"

Gideon shook his head. "The storm has gotten pretty bad. I suspect he's turned in for the night."

"Do you think he was looking for the drugs?"

He raised his shoulders in a careless shrug. "I wouldn't be surprised."

"I was going to mention this earlier, but I didn't want to alarm the kids any more than they already were. There were two guys in a tan SUV following us from Iowa. I saw their faces when we stopped for gas. I'm not sure if it was an accident or on purpose, but their vehicle almost pinned me against the van. And then, later, they may have bumped us off the road."

Gideon remained quiet for a moment, and when he spoke, his voice was soft and measured. "You may be right about that. I saw an SUV that matched that description idling on the road when Lou and I were checking the perimeter."

Dani could hardly contain her excitement.

"That makes sense. They were probably waiting for me to leave so they could unload the cocaine and transport it to the reservation."

He nodded his head. "It's a possibility."

A possibility? This new information was a game changer. Didn't it prove her innocence beyond a shadow of a doubt? But then why was Gideon acting so reserved?

The room seemed strangely quiet, the only noise being the sound of the boys' hoarse breathing. She stared out the window at the dark stretch of night. "Do you have any idea how long it will take to get all of us across the lake? There's some sort of luncheon planned at the rec center, and I was wondering if we'll make it in time to attend."

Gideon shot her an inscrutable look. "There are eight of you, and that means eight trips, at least fifteen minutes each way. It's not ideal, but it's the only option we've got at the moment." He reached down and scratched Lou's belly. "The kids should arrive in time for lunch, but the sheriff may need you to stick around to answer a few questions."

She nodded to show that she understood, but she didn't. Gideon had seen the men in the tan SUV. They were probably the ones who had planted the drugs and implicated her in the process. Why wasn't he concerned about that?

"I don't know what more I can say about any of this." Her eyes filled with tears as she thought about being interrogated by the sheriff. What sort of information could she offer that would be any different than what she had already told Gideon? "I just want it all to be over and for the kids to be safe."

Gideon reached down and patted Lou on the head. "This is an extremely volatile situation, Dani. Law enforcement is totally committed to solving the problems of addiction that have been plaguing the community. Cal's not going to leave a single stone unturned until he gets to the bottom of this."

She nodded. "I understand that. But you'll be with me when I talk to the sheriff, right?"

"I can make sure he knows about the SUV. But you need to understand that I'm a civilian. And this smuggling operation is a lot more complicated than it seems at first glance."

A flush of heat warmed her cheeks. "Tell me, Gideon. Do I look like the kind of person who would drive a van five hundred miles across three state lines with a group of teenage kids and a trunk full of cocaine? I haven't done anything wrong, but you're acting like I'm a criminal."

A muscle tensed in Gideon's jaw. "I'm sorry you think that." He turned back toward the window and resumed his watch.

She walked into the bedroom and closed the door. Hot tears stung her eyes as she sank back against the cool cotton cloth of the pillowcase and tried to calm her mind.

It had been presumptuous to assume that Gideon was on her side. In a few hours' time, she would talk to the sheriff and tell him the truth— that she didn't have any idea how the drugs got into the van. There was no reason to suspect that he wouldn't believe her, even if Gideon had his doubts.

The main thing she needed at the moment was sleep. But even as she finally drifted off, she did so with a sense of foreboding that dark and dreadful forces were gathering against her in the night.

FOUR

The alarm on her phone sounded just a few minutes after six.

Stumbling half-asleep into the main room, Dani was surprised to see a pot of coffee on the stove, a blazing fire in the hearth and a line of cereal boxes on the counter.

There was a shuffling sound behind her, and she turned to find that she was no longer alone in the kitchen. "What's Mr. Marshall doing outside?" Lucy asked, pointing through the window at a dark figure moving slowly across the yard. Backlit by a full moon, Gideon appeared to be shoveling a two-foot-wide pathway to the barn.

"He must be getting things ready to take us across the lake."

Dani looked out the window again. It was still dark, with only a thin gray line hinting at the possibility of dawn. She could see Gideon wielding his shovel with the precision of a well-oiled machine. Watching him work made her ashamed of her outburst the night before. She had crossed the line in asking for his protection and support. He had done so much for her already. In comparison, her job was easy. She just had to make sure everyone was ready at their designated departure time and to straighten up the cabin before they all left.

And she did. One by one, the kids headed out the door and climbed aboard the snowmobile with Gideon at the helm. And just like that, the process was repeated six more times until she was the only one left at the cabin.

The memory of the gunshot continued to trouble her thoughts as she busied herself tidying up. As it turned out, she had plenty of time to wash the dishes, clean the kitchen and sweep the dining room floor. She had just finished changing the linens on the bed when she realized it was well past the time that Gideon ought to have returned. What was taking so long? The first six trips had gone like clockwork, so she expected the same when Gideon left with Josh. That was close to ten thirty, and now it was—what? —the clock on the stove indicated that more than a full hour had passed since their departure.

She paced off the distance to the window and peered outside. It was unsettling to be alone in the cabin. Of course, she still had Lou, who was somewhere outside "guarding the perimeter," to use Gideon's fanciful description. She had been glad when he decided to leave the shepherd in the yard rather than inside the cabin. Lou was probably a very nice dog, once you got to know him, but he had a huge mouth full of pointed teeth and a bark that was sharp and explosive.

Not to mention the fact that he seemed to hold her responsible for all the problems she had caused for his master. Every time he marched by the window on his patrol, he'd glance inside and give her a dirty look. Actually, now that she thought about it, she hadn't seen his scowling face for quite some time, which was odd, since she had spent the last ten minutes scanning the horizon in hopes of spotting the snowmobile heading for shore.

What was the weight limit on one of those things, anyway? Josh was a tall boy and Gideon was no lightweight, so it was well within the realm of possibility that the overburdened vehicle had crashed through the ice. Dani shook her head to dislodge the image of the two males, their clothing heavy and waterlogged, trying to scramble out of the frozen lake. It was too terrible a thought to contemplate, and she closed her eyes and said a prayer that God would keep them safe.

She tried to picture the scene at the sheriff's office, where the kids would be gathered waiting for her to arrive. There were still so many arrangements to make. If the cell towers were working, she could've gotten a head start on her task list as she waited for Gideon, but the last time she'd checked her phone, there was still no service.

It was frustrating. And now, to add to her distress, the sound of frantic barking was coming from somewhere outside in the yard. She tried to convince herself that Lou was probably hot on the trail of a fox or a squirrel, but, given the shepherd's elite training, that seemed unlikely. What if he was sounding the alarm because Gideon and Josh had fallen through the ice? At this very moment, they could be struggling to reach shore, soaked and freezing. She looked out the window, but there was still no sign of movement on the lake. But the trees obstructed part of her view, and Lou was still barking. She needed a closer look.

She slipped into her coat and cracked open the door. A strong west wind nudged a layer of snow across the threshold, causing a momentary distraction. Before she could react, a man in a navy windbreaker stepped out from the shrubbery and placed a thick gloved hand over her face.

Terror welled inside her throat. She opened her mouth to scream, but her words were muffled against the fabric of his glove.

The behemoth's hand clamped down hard on her mouth, his fingers squeezing her nostrils until she couldn't breathe. She flailed against her attacker, but with her body being deprived of oxygen, her limbs felt heavy and sluggish. A darkness at the edge of her consciousness loomed ever closer. A few more seconds, and she would pass out.

A sudden flash of movement close to the ground caused her assailant to startle and loosen his grip.

Lou! Teeth barred, the shepherd hurled himself forward and clamped his jaw down on her assailant's leg.

She saw her opportunity. Pushing her elbows out, she twisted her body from his grip.

"Get off me." The man tried to shake the snarling dog off his pant leg with no success. "Vern." His voice came out in a strangled cry. "Get over here and shoot this crazy animal before he bites clear through the bone in my leg."

She looked at Lou. His dark eyes met hers with a message that was clear. *I've got this.* That might be true, but only until "Vern" arrived with a gun.

The man reached down and pulled a knife from an ankle holster on his free leg. "Let's see who's in charge now," he roared as he took a few swipes that missed. Lou yanked his head from side to side, avoiding the blade and maintaining his hold.

It was only a matter of time before the knife hit its mark. Or until Vern arrived on the scene. As she looked around for something she could use as a weapon, her eyes fell upon a half-split log beside the door. It was heavy, but she lifted it up and brought it down hard on her assailant's head. But not before the blade of his knife sliced through the flesh on the shepherd's leg.

Even then, Lou did not relinquish his grip. Only a whimper escaped through his clenched jaw as the man staggered backward, stunned by the blow.

There wasn't a moment to waste. "Lou!" She tilted her head toward the door of the cabin. "Go inside. Now."

Lou released his hold and limped across the threshold, collapsing in a heap on the floor. Dani rushed to slam the door behind him, turning the lock with shaking hands. They were safe for the moment, but for how long?

She struggled to control her breathing as she knelt to examine Lou's leg. He appeared to be in shock as he groaned with pain.

"No worries, boy. I'll take care of you." Her eyes darted left and right as hard fists pounded on the cabin's front door. The banging stopped, but a second later, a face appeared at the window that looked out over the lake. Without stopping to think, she ran across the room and picked up the crossbow. With trembling fingers, she felt for the trigger and pointed at the glass. Her heart thudded in her chest as she stared at the intruder. For the span of ten seconds, he glared back at her, and then he disappeared into the shadows. A plaintive whine pulled her attention back to the wounded shepherd. She peeled her fingers from the crossbow, set it down and took a deep breath. She couldn't give in to panic. She couldn't allow herself to think about anything but taking care of Lou.

She rubbed her hands together to regain circulation and bent to begin her examination. Lou's fur was sticky with fresh blood, and a thin red puddle had pooled under his leg. A look of pain clouded his dark eyes. But there was satisfaction there, too, at the success of a job well-done.

"I'm sorry you got hurt trying to protect me," she whispered, scratching his ears. Lou looked so vulnerable that she forgot to feel afraid. "You just lie here and wait while I find something to disinfect your leg."

Now, where would Gideon keep his first-aid kit? She checked the bathroom cabinet, but finding that stocked with toiletries—soap, deodorant, an unused can of shaving cream—she began a search of the vanity. In the bottom drawer, she found a small box containing Band-Aids, gauze and a bottle of antiseptic, and she set to work bandaging Lou's leg.

Just as she finished her ministrations, the shepherd's ears perked up, and the hair on the back of his neck bristled. Someone or something was outside the cabin. Her first thought was to hide, but she felt cowardly abandoning Lou. Beside her, his tail twitched in expectation. Had the men returned? Once again, she reached for the crossbow and waited.

The key turned in the lock, and Gideon walked inside. Her fingers flinched, and she set down the weapon, relief firing through her senses. Gideon's eyes landed on his wounded pet. "What happened?"

"Lou was barking so I went outside to investigate. A man was waiting, and he tried to suffocate me. He probably would have succeeded if it hadn't been for Lou. He bit the guy. And I hit him with a piece of wood."

"Are you okay?"

Her breath hitched. "I'm fine. Lou took the brunt of the attack."

"How many of them were there?"

"I only saw one, but I heard him shout to his friend."

"I need to go look around." Gideon made a move to stand but lost his grip on the table and reached to steady himself against her arm. Exhaustion etched deep lines in his face, and his hand shook when he gripped her elbow to keep himself from falling onto the floor. There was no way he was capable of taking anyone on, especially a knife-wielding intruder.

"How about something warm to drink before you go out?"

"Maybe just some water," he said.

She filled a glass from the tap and handed it to him. "You were gone so long I was afraid that something had happened to you on the lake."

"We broke down about a half mile from shore, and Josh and I walked the rest of the way in."

"So, the kids are all safe?" Dani searched his eyes for reassurance.

"They're fine. When I left the station, the receptionist was arranging for a ride to the reservation."

"What will happen to your snowmobile?"

"I left it out on the lake. It was on its last legs, anyway. With the storm picking back up, we'll be stuck at the cabin for another night. But the sheriff knows we're out here, so as soon as the snow stops, he'll send someone to pick us up."

"What about Lou?"

Gideon shrugged. "Twenty-four hours shouldn't make that much of a difference in getting him to the vet, especially since you did a good job of dressing the wound. There's nothing we can do at this point except to keep him comfortable."

"And the drugs?"

A shadow passed over Gideon's face. "Locked in a safe at the sheriff's station."

Dani blanched. "I assume there's no way the intruders know that."

"Anyone who's interested will find out soon enough. Multiply seven kids by two deputies and a half-dozen administrators at the reservation. Word gets out fairly quickly around these parts."

At least that was what he was hoping. He set down his glass and prepared once again to brave the minus-twenty-degree windchill. As he reached for the crossbow and slung it over his shoulder, Lou opened one eye and made a feeble attempt to stand. The sight of his wounded pet struggling was like a kick to the stomach. Rage surged through him as he thought of the thug who had attacked Dani and stabbed Lou. His first priority tomorrow would be to get Dani to the sheriff's office and his dog to the vet.

A crack of wind struck him across the face as he opened the door to the cabin. It took all his willpower not to stop and inspect Lou's wounded leg, but securing the perimeter was his first priority.

Lou had been with him almost from the start

of Gideon's career at the DEA. He remembered the first time they met at a training facility in Florida. Still a young puppy, Lou was a bundle of pure energy and downy fur. But it didn't take long for him to learn that he was cut out for bigger things than just eating and sleeping. His calm temperament and tenacious personality made it easy for him to learn the ropes on the job. And it wasn't long before he became a canine superstar. Among the team of agents, Lou definitely pulled his own weight, all seventy-seven pounds of him.

Gideon had to hand it to Dani. He had recognized right away that she was frightened by the big dog, but when push came to shove, she'd come through for Lou. Of course, that didn't mean he had changed his mind about sticking his nose into the investigation. He hadn't. He stood by what he'd said the night before when they'd discussed her upcoming meeting with the sheriff. Dani might not agree with his position, but he wouldn't interfere. Cal was in charge. It was as simple as that. Besides, Dani didn't need him to be her advocate. She just had to go in there and tell the truth.

Last night, it had taken all the self-control he could muster to avoid a discussion about the tan SUV. The last thing he wanted to do was offer

Dani false hope about the significance of the new information.

In any case, he couldn't worry about Dani's defense strategy right now. He just had to keep her safe. Pushing open the barn door, he made a beeline toward the place he stored his trusty Louisville Slugger. The wooden bat made a satisfying thwack as he smacked it against the palm of his glove. Along with the crossbow, it would have to do as he scouted the perimeter, though he couldn't help thinking that that his old Sig P220 would've come in handy at a time like this. His decision to turn in his guns had seemed like a sensible one at the time. But the two years he had spent in Dagger Lake had brought a lot of healing. Maybe, when this whole mess got sorted out, he'd buy himself a shotgun. But for now, he had a baseball bat.

It galled him to think of all that cocaine being targeted for delivery to the reservation. It was the last thing the tribe needed, with all the problems already in the mix. The last year had been an especially hard one for everyone in Dagger Lake. Early spring's floodwaters had destroyed dozens of buildings and homes, and the folks on the reservation had suffered even more than most. Families had lost a lifetime of possessions, and few had the resources to rebuild and start again. Many had just pulled up stakes and moved away.

Well, he wasn't going anywhere. This was his home. It wasn't an easy truth, but it was one he had come to accept. He had spent too long searching for a place to belong, and Dagger Lake held a lot of memories. Some good. Some bad. And some he was still trying to understand.

He made his way past the house on his first loop around the property. The drifting snow almost completely covered the intruders' tracks, and only a log on the ground by the front door remained as testament of the struggle that had taken place. It was hard to believe that the man who had attacked Dani had been scared off by a simple blow to the head. Unless she had hit him harder than she thought. In any case, it was a relief that the drugs were no longer on the premises. In his experience, bad people generally went away once you no longer had what they wanted. But in this case, he wasn't so sure that would be true.

The way he saw it, Dani had been targeted as a mule to transport the cocaine to the reservation. A van driven by a youth group leader at a church—what could be more innocent than that? Of course, there was one small snag in that theory. The sheriff had let slip that his office had received an early tip about a consignment of drugs coming into the area, and that information threw a whole new wrinkle into the mix.

He tried to make sense of it, but his mind was dull from exhaustion. Circling past the barn, he noticed that a few of the shingles on the roof had blown off in the storm, and he made a mental note to replace them when the weather improved. And after he did that, he should probably check that the cabin had not sustained damage, as well. It made his bones feel weary just to think about it. It had been a long, grueling day, beginning in the early hours of the morning with the first of seven trips across the lake. By the time it had been Josh's turn, his hands were shaking from the cold and the vibrations from the machine. And walking back through the drifts with the ice pelting his face had been rough. No wonder he was so tired that he could hardly stand.

But tomorrow would be another day. The weather seemed to be easing up, so there was reason to hope that the roads would soon be open and clear. In the morning he'd use the sat phone Cal gave him at the station and arrange a time for someone to pick them up.

Gideon closed his eyes and imagined a best-case scenario for the day ahead. For Dani, a quick interview with the sheriff and a ride out to the reservation. For Lou, a bandaged leg and a well-deserved nap in front of the fire. And for himself? Nothing more than a return to the simple life he had been leading before a dark-haired woman with sparkling eyes turned his world upside down.

FIVE

Gideon's freezer was a treasure trove of weirdly shaped packages without dates or identifying marks.

She couldn't remember the last time she had cooked an entire meal from scratch. Maybe Christmas three years ago, when her parents came to dinner at her apartment? Her foray into gourmet cuisine had involved a box of noodles, a can of spaghetti sauce and a pot of boiling water. And the compliments she had received for her efforts had been nothing short of astonishing.

Apparently, her folks had been expecting something a whole lot worse.

And, really, who could blame them? During a typical workweek, she subsisted on a diet of fast food, Chinese takeout and ready-to-eat entrées from the grocery store. It wasn't that she hated to cook. She just didn't have the time. Her job at the lab required her to work long hours, and any free time she had after that was spent volunteering with the youth group at the church.

But cooking was a way to stay busy. Anything to occupy her mind as she waited for Gideon to return. And, as scary as the situation was, they needed to eat.

"Something smells good." Gideon stomped the ice off his boots as he walked through the door. The shoulders of his parka were covered with a cement-like coating of frozen snow, and his face was flushed from the cold.

"Um…thanks?" She glanced at the pot of stew bubbling on the stovetop. The scent could more accurately be described as pungent, and given the strange mixture of ingredients—a pound of ground meat, a can of tomato soup, a packet of chicken broth and a jar of creamed corn—she just hoped it was edible.

Gideon kicked off his boots and walked into the kitchen, his two big toes poking through holes in his striped wool socks. He looked strangely vulnerable in his stocking feet and maybe just a bit adorable as he walked across the room and knelt down to pet Lou. "How's the patient doing?"

"Pretty good. Lots of moaning and groaning, but he's sleeping a lot, too."

Gideon scratched the dog behind the ears and then straightened and hobbled toward the table.

She dished portions of stew into two blue earthenware bowls. At the sight of the irregular bits of hamburger floating in the thin gravy, her appetite took a nosedive, but Gideon appeared to have no such compunctions as he lifted his spoon and prepared to dig in.

"Shall I say the prayer, or will you?" she asked.

"You go ahead." He set his spoon down beside his plate and waited.

She closed her eyes. "Father God, we thank You for this day and for the food that is before us. Thank You also for keeping the kids and Gideon safe under Your protection. For all these things, in Your name we pray. Amen."

Gideon waited for the prayer to end before lifting the spoon to his lips.

The hamburger stew wasn't half-bad, especially when she sopped it up with a piece of bread. The recipe might not be fancy enough for the Food Network, but it was filling and reasonably nutritious. Gideon was even hungrier than she was. He helped himself to seconds and scraped the last bits from the bottom of his bowl. He wiped his mouth with his napkin and turned to offer her an appreciative smile.

"That was delicious. Thanks." He leaned forward in an expectant way that made it clear he had something more on his mind than complimenting the chef. With the yellow cone of the kitchen light shining directly into her face, the scene was set for another interrogation. "I was hoping we could talk about your case."

Her case? She thought he wasn't interested. In any event, she definitely did not like the direction the conversation was heading. Was he getting ready to play good cop or bad cop? It was hard to tell from his expression. Though his tone was mild, her heart started to hammer at the implication of his words.

"Can you tell me again what happened when the intruder attacked you this morning?" he asked.

She nodded. "I heard Lou barking, and I went outside to see if it was you. A man stepped from the shadows and put his hand over my face." She shivered, recalling the terror of not being able to breathe. "Lou arrived just as I was about to lose consciousness. He bit the man's leg and distracted him so that I could get away."

"Did you see your attacker's face?"

"Just for a moment. He had short hair and a scar on his forehead over his left brow. And when Lou came to my rescue, he called out for someone named Vern to shoot the dog."

"You didn't see a gun?"

"No, just a knife. Is it possible that those men

were scoping out the cabin because they assumed that the drugs were still in my possession?"

Gideon raised a skeptical brow, but what else made sense? She could only pray that now that the cocaine was locked in the sheriff's safe, the men would leave them alone.

"It may be more complicated than that," he said. "When I was in town, the sheriff mentioned that they had received an anonymous tip about a van with Iowa plates transporting a shipment of cocaine to the reservation."

She squinted in confusion. Did this mean they were dealing with two different groups—one who hid the drugs in the van and another who wanted them discovered? "So even if Lou hadn't found the cocaine, the police would have stopped us when we got to the reservation?"

"Sounds like it." Gideon brought a hand to his temple and massaged his forehead. "Listen, Dani. I've been thinking about our conversation last night. And I want to explain why I can't get personally involved in this case. When I retired from the DEA, I made a couple of vows about how I wanted to live my life, and so far, I've been able to keep them. The first was to keep my nose out of other people's business. Cal's the head lawman of Dagger Lake County, and what he says goes. It's not my place to tell him how to do his job."

"I wasn't asking you to interfere with the investigation."

"I understand. But I can't make a promise I can't keep. That was the second vow I made when I turned in my badge. And at this point, with so many complicating factors in the mix, I can't really speculate since I don't know how it's all going down."

"Okay." She didn't know what else she could say. Gideon had done so much for her and the kids already. She had been out of line asking for more.

"One thing I can do is make sure you go into your interview with the sheriff knowing what to expect. He's going to ask you a lot of questions, and you'll need to dig deep and think about everything that happened in the days leading up to the mission trip. Maybe even go beyond that to consider things that may have happened in the past."

She studied the man sitting across from her. Weariness was etched into the lines of his face, and his eyes were smudged from lack of sleep. What could she say except to repeat again that she led a simple life, dividing her time between work and her volunteer duties at the church?

A life that was nothing out of the ordinary. Except for one thing.

"I had a twin sister who was abducted and murdered when we were thirteen," she said. Then she waited for the usual response.

"I'm sorry." His eyes darkened with pity.

"Thanks." She gave the standard reply. Fifteen years of practice had made her familiar with the routine.

Would she ever be allowed to forget that windy March day when life as she knew it came to an end? An ordinary day in an ordinary week, when the most exciting item on the agenda was the dance coming up that weekend at school.

For a long time, she had felt guilty. It had been her idea to bake the cookies, forgetting to check if all the ingredients were on hand. She was the one who suggested that they ride their bikes to the store. And she was the one who slowed down to a stop when the man approached them from the trees.

Identical twins. One is taken, and the other is spared.

Three weeks after the kidnapping, her sister's body was discovered in a Dumpster two miles from their parents' home. Three long weeks of waiting, of staying home from school, unable to read or watch TV, praying that Ali might still be alive. Her parents had tried to hide the specifics from her, but all the grisly details of the crime were splashed across the front pages of the newspaper.

Death by strangulation.

When she thought about that, she could almost feel the man's fingers squeezing her own throat as he choked the life from his sister. A few more weeks passed. And then, finally, the police made an arrest. She remembered the detective in charge of the investigation telling her parents that they'd been able to match a sample found on her sister's body to the suspect's DNA. Because of advances in forensic science, Ali's killer would spend the rest of his life in jail.

"Dani?" Gideon's voice pulled her back from her memories. "Are you okay?"

"I am. I was just thinking about how I used to believe that the man who murdered my sister was coming back to get me. Even after he was caught and sent to jail, I worried that he'd escape and find me as he had threatened during the trial. My parents urged me to talk to a counselor, and I did. He showed me pictures of the prison where Ali's killer was being held and pointed out all the barbed wire on top of the fences and the towers with armed guards. It helped. But sometimes I still dream that he's out there, waiting for me."

Gideon nodded. "When you tell Cal about

your sister, he'll check to make sure her murderer is still in jail. That will be his first priority. But if that doesn't pan out, he'll need to look elsewhere for answers. What about your job?"

"It's nothing exciting. I'm a scientist. I work in a lab."

"Any chance you just discovered a new wonder drug?"

She shook her head, glad for a change of subject. "I'm not that kind of scientist. I work in a lab, but I don't do research or perform product trials. I test DNA."

His eyes registered interest. "Okay, good. There might be something to that. Tell me more."

She looked down at the table, suddenly self-conscious about the less-than-exciting aspects of her job. "Mostly I do paternity testing."

He leaned forward and stroked his head. With his strong arms and muscular frame, he looked less like a wild mountain man than an NFL quarterback, and she forced her eyes to turn away.

"But you also do crime scene analysis?"

"Not as much as the other stuff, but we do work for a number of police departments in the area. We won an award last year as one of the top forensic labs in the country."

She waited for the next question. But he pushed back his chair and stood up from the table. "That might be something the sheriff will want to dig into. Knowing Cal, I suspect he'll probably have some of his own ideas on the subject." He reached across the table for her silverware and bowl.

Apparently, Gideon had decided it was time to do the dishes.

Fifteen minutes later, she hung up the dish towel and turned to face him. He was slumped against the refrigerator, his eyes half-closed. A pang of tenderness welled in her heart. "You must be dead on your feet. Let's call it a night."

Once again, Gideon insisted on bunking on the couch, claiming he wanted to keep an eye on Lou. More likely, he was worried that the intruders might return to the cabin. After washing up, she climbed into bed and pulled the blankets tight against her chest. She hadn't expected to fall asleep, but with all the stress and anxiety, she was out the minute her head hit the pillow. Four hours later, she woke up to the sound of a ringing phone, one of those jazzy little riffs that added to the confusion of interrupted sleep. Her first thought was that the cell towers were finally back up, but when she checked her own phone, there was still no reception.

Through a crack in the door, she could hear strains of a muffled conversation. It sounded like Gideon was engaged in a fairly contentious discussion with the person at the other end of the line. When she heard her name mentioned, she stepped out to investigate.

Gideon stood by the window, phone to his ear, staring out into the wide starless night. He cut a daunting figure when seen in the dim living room. It was strange being stranded in a cabin with a retired federal agent, but the fact that he was tall and handsome complicated things that much more.

She felt her cheeks redden as he turned and saw her watching him. He held up two fingers to show that he was almost finished and then swiveled sideways and lowered his voice.

"Okay… Okay." She strained to hear him. "Sure… I get it… Yes, of course… I'll see you then, okay?" He slipped the sat phone into the pocket of his sweatpants and then looked over to meet her curious stare. "Sorry if I woke you up. I meant to turn the ringer down before I went to bed."

"I thought the phones weren't working and that the towers were down." Her voice sounded petulant even to her own ears.

"They are. This one works on a satellite signal. Cal lent it to me when I was at the station."

She tilted her head sideways and gave him a curious look. "Was that the sheriff you were just talking to on the phone?"

"It was."

He didn't elaborate. It didn't look like he was going to tell her why the sheriff had called him this late at night. And he didn't seem to want to chat about anything else, either.

"Well, I guess I'll head back to bed," she said.

"Great."

Yeah, great. She turned and slipped through the bedroom door. She felt disappointed, but, really, what was she expecting? Did she imagine that Gideon would ask her to pull up a chair so that they could continue their discussion about the drugs? That didn't seem likely. His face was fixed in a resolute expression, and he seemed determined to play his cards close to the vest.

Gideon waited until Dani stepped out of the room before adjusting the ringer on his phone. He had been speaking in a low tone so she probably hadn't overheard much of his conversation with the sheriff. But judging from the anxious expression on her face, she'd heard enough.

No way could he tell her the reason for Cal Stanek's call. It would only make her more upset. Apparently, another bag of cocaine had been discovered in the parking lot outside a church in Blooming Prairie, Iowa, on the front seat of a 2011 sky blue Nissan registered to Danika Audrey Jones. The lead had come from yet another anonymous tip.

Maybe it was the skeptic in him, but something about this new lead didn't pass the smell test. In his fifteen years with the DEA, he had dealt with a lot of criminals who would lie, cheat and even kill to further their ambitions. Some were careless, and some were arrogant, but he'd never met anyone who would leave a packet of cocaine in plain sight in a car. Under the seat or in the glove box, maybe, but not right out in the open for any passerby to see. Of course, drug users did dumb things, especially while impaired. And Dani had certainly seemed dazed and distracted when she stepped out of the van and later, in the barn when he had questioned her about the cocaine.

But this latest discovery pushed the envelope too far. He balked at being force-fed information and led by his nose toward a foregone conclusion. In fact, this latest campaign to implicate Dani was having the opposite effect for him. He was beginning to think that Dani Jones was exactly the person she claimed to be—a young woman who liked her job, loved her family and enjoyed helping kids. The most unique thing about her involved an incident that had taken place years in the past—the murder of her twin sister. At the DEA, he hadn't dealt directly with that sort of crime, but he had seen firsthand how murder could rip a family apart and leave a path of destruction in its wake. It had torn at his heart to see Dani's face crumple when she shared her fears that Ali's killer was still out there, waiting to hurt her as he had hurt her sister.

Gideon might never understand the depth of Dani's pain, but he was well versed in the heartbreak of loss. His mother had never recovered from his father's death, and he could only imagine that the loss of an identical twin would cut all the deeper. But he would stake his reputation on the fact that the man who'd murdered Ali was not the person they were looking for. The psychological profile didn't fit. The planted drugs, the attempts on Dani's life, the hired thugs—they didn't seem like the MO of a deranged murderer. They were more like... He rubbed his eyes. The answer was out there, just beyond his reach. But couldn't put his finger on it. Beside the couch, Lou twitched on his bed and snored in his sleep. He was probably dreaming about chasing squirrels, forgetting that he had a large white bandage wrapped around his leg.

Two days ago, their life had been fairly routine. Get up in the morning, eat breakfast, do chores, have lunch, chop some wood and then more chores until it was time for dinner. Of course, there'd be the occasional coyote who wandered onto the property, sending Lou into paroxysms of delight. But nothing like this.

The irony of the situation was not lost on him. Just last night, he had told Dani that she needed to allow the legal system to work. He had stared straight into those guileless gray eyes of hers and insisted that he could not—would not—get involved. But the more he thought about it, the more his resolve wavered. Conflicting emotions raced across his brain as he reviewed the facts as he knew them.

Someone had planted the drugs, either to smuggle them into the reservation or to frame Dani. Assuming the first possibility, how to explain the anonymous tips that pointed authorities in Dani's direction? But if it was all an elaborate frame job, then the person who planted the drugs certainly had cash to spare. A million dollars was a heavy price tag for a setup. And then there were the attacks on Dani's life that had come in waves and taken the form of a hastily conceived plan B. There was no doubt that someone wanted Dani dead. But why was it important that she also be caught smuggling cocaine? Who stood to gain if Dani was out of the picture and her reputation was in tatters?

But asking the questions didn't change what came next. He had promised Cal that he would bring Dani in for questioning, and, like it or not, that was what he would do. He looked out the window at the elm tree clinging to the snowy lakeshore. The floodwaters had reached a high mark on its battered trunk, but its deep, thick roots kept it anchored to the earth. At the moment, he felt as worn-out and tired as that old elm. He just needed to continue holding on until Dani was safe and the men who tried to hurt her were brought to justice. Then, he could go back to the way things were before he stumbled upon the van in the ditch, before he found the drugs, before the gunshots and men in the tan SUV. And before he met Dani Jones.

SIX

Lou opened his eyes at the first sign of dawn, whimpering softly as he struggled to pull himself upright on his injured leg. Gideon carried him outside to do his business and refilled his bowls with water and chow.

He was making coffee when Dani joined him in the kitchen. She was wearing jeans and a plaid shirt, and she had pulled her long brown tresses into a high ponytail. She looked so pretty and fresh that it took his breath away. To keep from gawking, he grabbed a pair of mugs and set them on the counter. Best to not let her see the effect she was having on him.

He thought about apologizing again for the midnight interruption but decided the less said about that the better. His goal today was to get Dani to town so she could talk to the sheriff. The worst of the storm had passed, and the two thugs from the SUV would be looking to make a move. It was no longer safe for her to stay at the cabin.

"How did you sleep?" she asked.

"Pretty good." In truth, he had tossed and turned until exhaustion overcame the mental gymnastics his mind wanted to play on the subject of Dani Jones.

He made a show of checking the water tank on the coffee maker. Anything to avoid meeting Dani's eyes.

"Gideon?" Dani said. "It smells like something is burning. I thought the coffee had boiled over. But it seems a lot stronger than that."

As soon as she said it, he noticed it, too. The acrid smell of scorched wood was faint but unmistakable. He opened the door. Gray smoke was pouring from the crossbars of the barn. The same barn he had designed and built with his own hands, using wood from the trees on his property and a lot of blood, sweat and tears.

He grabbed his parka and rushed outside with Dani following close behind. She didn't stop to put on her coat, so she shivered noticeably in spite of the blaze.

"Do you have an extinguisher? Or maybe a hose we can hook up to a spigot?" She raised her voice to be heard over the crackling fire.

He shook his head. There was nothing to be done. The portable fire extinguisher he kept in the closet would be ineffective against a blaze of this size. And water from the garden hose would freeze before it reached the nozzle.

Sparks flew all around them, sizzling as they landed on the cold snow. A sudden shift in the wind rained ashes down on their shoulders, and noxious plumes of smoke curled around their heads.

Dani covered her eyes and started to cough. A desperate feeling of urgency spurred him into action. The left wall of the structure was fully engulfed in flames, and an ominous creaking hinted at an imminent collapse. It wouldn't take much for the fire to jump from the barn to the house. This wasn't an accident. His gut told him the fire had been deliberately set to draw them outside and that the men were lurking somewhere nearby, hoping for a clear shot at Dani.

"Go inside and wait with Lou." He directed his plea to Dani.

"Okay." Her voice quaked, but her movements didn't seem to register the immediacy of his request.

"Go now, Dani," he said. "Run."

She turned and sprinted toward the cabin, pausing when she reached the door. She looked back over her shoulder and shouted, "Don't worry about Lou. I'll make sure he doesn't get too scared."

"Get inside! Now!"

Relief flooded his senses as she darted into the cabin, slamming the door.

Not a moment too soon.

A thumping blast echoed from somewhere on his left, and a fraction of a second later, a spray of shotgun pellets splintered sharp groves in the wooden front door.

Gideon crouched down and assumed a defensive position. Dani was safe—that was the important thing—but the thugs were out there, even closer than he had thought.

Inside the cabin, Dani paced the twenty-foot distance from the window to the door, stopping every few minutes to reassure Lou.

Ten minutes passed, and Gideon walked into the room. His eyes were red and irritated, and his parka was covered with filmy gray soot. He held a finger to his lips as he moved across the room, flicking off the light switches and pulling the shades.

He handed her a flashlight and motioned toward the bedroom door. "We need to leave here now. The wind is changing, and the fire could spread to the cabin. Grab your coat and purse, but leave the rest of your stuff for later. In the closet, there's a door to the basement. Go down the stairs and wait for me. I'll get Lou and meet you at the bottom."

It wasn't the time to ask any of the questions flashing through her brain. Pulling on her coat and picking up her handbag, she hurried into the bedroom and opened the panel on the closet floor. The beam of her flashlight illuminated the rough edges of a set of dusty wooden stairs. Her fingers trembling as she gripped the sides of the wall, she began her descent into the dark cellar, each step creaking menacingly under her feet.

A musty scent assailed her nostrils, and dampness chilled her bones. Training her light on the earthen walls, she surveyed the space, pausing to let the light play over a wide section of pipe that looked like it had been abandoned halfway through installation. The ceiling shuddered with noises from above, and next to her feet, a mouse skidded boldly across the packed clay floor. She put her hand over her mouth to keep from screaming. Panic shook her, and she did what she had always done in the past when she felt alone and afraid. She closed her eyes and prayed. Though anxious and powerless, she reminded herself that God was beside her, as He had been with her during all of her days.

Moments later, she heard the clank of the trapdoor opening, followed by the sound of heavy footsteps on the stairs. She bit back panic until she saw a familiar figure hurrying toward her with Lou in his arms. Gideon. At last. On his forehead was a bright orange headlamp, and under his arm was a folded tarp. The stiff plastic crackled as he shook it out and set the frightened dog on top.

"I bought a line of pipe when I built the cabin in order to lay a tunnel to the garage."

She eyed the three-foot-wide opening with incredulity. Was this the tunnel he was talking about? It hardly looked big enough to accommodate an adult, let alone a man the size of Gideon.

He looped a section of rope around his waist and connected it to the bungee cord harness he'd wound through the grommets of the tarp. "I'll go first, since I'll be pulling Lou. It's about a hundred yards to the garage. When we get to the end, I'll open the latch and pull you through. All set?"

She nodded. She was as set as she'd ever be, as long as she could ignore the rapid thumping of her heart in her chest.

"Be careful when you go over the seams. If you hit them hard, they can tear up your knees."

She tilted her beam toward the spot where Gideon was kneeling by the entrance to the pipe. He pushed himself forward with his hands, dragging Lou behind him like a child on a sled. She could just about see the light from his headlamp and Lou's glowing eyes as the tarp was swallowed up by the darkness.

She entered next. The pipe felt smooth and cold to the touch, and they made quick time for the first twenty or so yards. Gideon had been right to warn her about the rough spots where the sections were fused. The first time she banged her knee, a stabbing pain shot through her leg, causing her to gasp.

Gideon stopped. "You okay back there?"

"I'm fine." She rubbed her palm against her knee. It throbbed under the pressure of her fingertips, but the discomfort was nothing compared to the full-fledged panic attack that threatened to overtake her. Drawing in a deep breath, she inched her way forward through the pipe.

"We're almost halfway there." Gideon's tone was urgent as he called back to her. "Remember—slow and steady."

The second half of the journey took twice as long as the first. Gideon's pace had slowed markedly, and each inch of forward movement was followed by a long pause. At times, it felt like they were barely making progress at all. Lou turned his head to shoot her a worried look, and she knew that she needed to act brave, even if she had to fake it.

"It's okay, boy," she murmured softly.

And it was.

Just when it seemed like they would never reach the end, Gideon stretched forward and unlocked the latch. Minutes later, his strong arms lifted Lou up out of the pipe. He pulled himself through the opening and then bent down to help her.

As her hands touched the smooth cement of the garage floor, she was surprised by how cold it was, much chillier than it had been in the tunnel. But despite the blast of frigid air, it was a relief to finally stretch her legs and let them uncramp after forty minutes inside the pipe.

It took a minute for her eyes to become adjusted to the sunlight streaming through the side windows of the shed. The muscles in Gideon's arms strained as he carried Lou across the garage and set him down on the floor of the truck. From what she could see, the vehicle appeared to be in an advanced state of disrepair. The hood was open, and several important-looking hoses were dangling unmoored.

"Over by the window is an old ice chest full of tools." Gideon's voice beckoned from under the hood. "Dump it out and find me a clamp and a ratchet wrench." He seemed to suddenly remember his manners. "Please."

She bent down and searched the chest. Finding a gizmo that looked like a large version of a weapon from Clue, she offered it to Gideon, but he shook his head. There was one other tool that was wrench-like in shape, so she handed him that and hoped for the best.

"Perfect." He bent over to tighten a bolt. "This quick fix is going to destroy my engine. But there's not a lot I can do about that. If you open the garage door, I'll fire this baby up. If the roads aren't too bad, maybe we can make it to town in time for lunch."

SEVEN

After a series of worrisome coughs, the engine engaged, and the truck lurched out of the garage into the blinding light of a clear December day.

Dani took a deep breath to calm her racing heart. The men with the guns were out there somewhere, waiting and watching. Gideon's knuckles were white as he clutched the steering wheel and piloted their course through the drifts.

The driveway took a sharp bend around the side of the lake before disappearing under a canopy of soft pines. Feathery branches swept against the truck like a winter car wash whooshing away the dust even as rays of translucent sunshine cut ribbons through the treetops, offering occasional glimpses of a cobalt blue sky.

As they made the turn onto the main road, the wheels of the truck spun into the curve, jostling Lou sideways against the mat on the floor. The frightened dog raised his head and placed it on Dani's lap, his eyes liquid with pain. The trill of a siren resounded in the distance, and a moment later, a fire truck sped past them on the road.

"Took them long enough," Gideon said. "I called them from the cabin before I came down the stairs."

"Do you want to go back and see what's going on?"

He shook his head. "They'll have their hands full containing the blaze. I can only hope that the fire won't spread from the barn."

A ribbon of hopelessness clutched at her senses. Everything that had happened to Gideon could be traced directly to her arrival at his cabin. She hugged her arms tight around her chest as guilt pressed down on her, making her heart heavy with shame.

She took a deep breath. "You're probably wishing that you never took that walk across the road and saw our van go into that ditch."

A muscle in his jaw twitched as he met and held her gaze. "I told you before. I was glad to help. We made it this far without a problem. Let's focus on the positive for the rest of the drive into town."

Focus on the positive. She settled back against the rough, cracked leather and bit down hard on her lip to keep herself from crying. The events of the last two days seemed like a nightmare that only got worse with each passing hour.

Ahead of them, a battered old salt truck lumbered along slowly, spraying half circles of brownish pebbles in its wake. As she glanced out the window of the cab at the bleak, flat landscape of snow and ice, sadness crept through her consciousness. She wasn't prepared to face the sheriff's questions. And she wasn't ready to say goodbye to Gideon.

The thought surprised her, and she quickly dismissed it. Her life was a delicate balance of work, family and activities at the church, and she needed to keep it that way. Look what happened the last time she was preoccupied. She'd inadvertently loaded a million dollars' worth of cocaine into the back of the van.

No. She wasn't looking for a relationship. She had so many other more important things to do before she could give in to the pull of her heart. Ali's murder had convinced her to embark on a life filled with purpose. Falling in love was a distraction she couldn't afford.

Her one and only serious boyfriend had resented her drive and single-minded focus. More than once during their long and painful breakup, he'd accused her of putting him last on her priority list, somewhere after her volunteer activities and her job at the lab, and well below the memory of her dead sister. His words had hurt at the time, but she was honest enough to recognize the truth in his assessment.

Almost without warning, the scenery started to change. Billboard advertisements and bus stop signs began to appear on the sides of the road. They passed a small gas station with a convenience store huddled on one side. A sign blinked in the window. Open Twenty-Four Hours. Fresh Coffee and Rolls.

She shifted in her seat as they approached a blinking yellow light at the intersection. A bent sign indicated that a right turn would take them into the town of Dagger Lake; a left turn, toward the reservation.

"Gideon?" Dani leaned forward, taking care not to disturb Lou, who was curled up at her feet. "Can we make a quick stop at the reservation? I'd like to see the kids and make sure they're okay."

Gideon gave her a sharp sideways look as he shifted into second gear. "I thought we'd check in with the sheriff first."

"Right." She nodded. Check in with the sheriff. That sounded promising. More like a brief chat than the full-scale interrogation she had been envisioning. Her most recent to-do list popped up in her mind. After they met with the sheriff, she'd need to contact the parents and begin making arrangements for the drive home.

After all, she was still the chaperone. The kids had been on their own for almost twenty-four hours. It was time for her to take charge.

But still. It was hard not to worry about what lay ahead. "How long have you known Sheriff Stanek?" she asked.

"About two years. When he was elected last July, there were a few locals who didn't like a newcomer taking over the position. But he won fair and square. I certainly have never had an issue with him. I took him out on my boat a couple of times and showed him a few places where the trout tend to congregate. Not all of them, mind you." His lips bent in a quick smile. "I have to keep a few secrets to myself."

"But he's a nice guy?"

Gideon shook his head. "Not sure I'd use the word *nice* to describe Cal Stanek, but he'd be one of the first people I'd call if I had a problem, that's for sure."

Lying wasn't always a bad thing, he told himself as he turned onto Main Street. It was sometimes a means to achieving a greater good. At least that used to be his philosophy when he worked at the DEA. Besides, not keeping Dani in the loop about the drugs that had been found in her car in Iowa wasn't really lying. He hadn't actually told a fib. Just omitted a few key facts when they talked about her case.

He always tried to be up-front in his dealings with his friends.

And he owed a similar kind of loyalty to Dani. Hadn't they just spent an excruciatingly long time together crawling through a thirty-six-inch-wide pipe? And before that, she had saved his dog and dressed his wounds. Still, he had given the sheriff his word that he wouldn't mention any specific details of the case to Dani, and he intended to keep that promise as well as he could.

So why was he feeling such an awful sense of dread as they approached their destination?

The gears on his truck made a grinding sound as he backed into a space on the lakefront, just south of the municipal building at the corner of Fifth and Main. The ornate stone structure dated back to the 1920s, when mining companies were discovering hidden veins of silver and gold in the quarries outside the city. Those days had ended long ago, and now the two-story structure housed almost all of the city offices, as well as the police department.

Shifting into Park, Gideon turned toward Dani. "I'll leave the truck running with Lou inside while I walk you into the station. That way, the cab will stay warm, and the battery will keep its charge. I'll stick around to make the introductions and then I'll take off to drive Lou to the vet. Once the interview is over, Cal will arrange a ride for you to the reservation."

"Okay," she said. As she climbed out of the truck, he reached into the back of the cab for an old blanket to toss over Lou. Then he stepped onto the sidewalk and smiled at Dani.

"Depending what happens with Lou, I'll probably see you tonight at the ceremony."

It was far from a definite commitment, but it was the best he could do under the circumstances.

When they reached the main building, he held the door and waited for her to step inside. He knew the way, but he let Dani take the lead as they walked briskly toward the man in a tan uniform and wide brimmed hat, standing in front of an open door.

Cal Stanek in all of his old-school cowboy glory.

Cal reached out and shook his hand. "Glad you made it in, Gideon. I just got word that the fire in your barn is under control and that so far, no flames have spread to the cabin."

"Thanks." Gideon turned and nodded toward Dani. "Sheriff, this is Dani Jones. She has come here of her own free will to answer all your questions. She knows you have some questions and that the interview might take some time, but she's hoping to make it to the reservation today."

"Nice to meet you, Miss Jones." Cal Stanek pointed to the back of the room. "My notes are on my desk, so why don't the two of us head back there to have a little chat? Gideon, I assume you no longer have need of my satellite phone?"

"Sure," Gideon said, taking the phone out of his pocket and setting it on an empty desk.

The sheriff's department employed only a handful of employees who provided support for residents of the town and the adjacent fifty square miles of reservation land. Currently on staff were two full-time deputies, a part-time clerk and a receptionist, who handled the phone. But at the moment, Cal appeared to be the only one in the office. Dani looked up and met Gideon's eyes, a brave smile flickering briefly on her lips as she turned to follow the sheriff to the back of the room.

As Gideon watched her go, he wrestled with a sudden change of heart. Lou would be fine in the warm cab, but Dani needed him here. At least for a couple of minutes, until he was sure she was okay. He took a seat at a desk and swiveled sideways for a view of the interrogation.

Cal leaned forward, a predator-like smile on his face while Dani stared at the floor, nervously twirling her hair.

It was Tyrannosaurus Rex meets Snow White, without the support of even one of the dwarves.

A protective instinct surged through his body. He didn't suspect Cal of any role in the drug-smuggling scheme, but it couldn't hurt to be on guard. Sure, Cal was a friend. But so was Jonas, his partner in Miami, and look how that had turned out. He shifted his eyes back to the front of the desk. According to the brass nameplate affixed to the side, it belonged to Ray Faegre, Gideon's old high school nemesis who'd joined the force right after college. Piles of paperwork covered the space, and an assortment of half-full coffee cups weighed down stacks of thick files.

Amid the chaos, a bright yellow Post-it note caught his eye.

He lifted it up and looked at the letters and numbers scrawled on the bottom. RCV 665.

The license plate of the church van.

The reasonable explanation occurred to him first. Hadn't Cal told him that an anonymous tip had come in about a vehicle smuggling drugs onto the reservation? It was possible that Deputy Faegre had taken the call and jotted down the details.

But why was the note buried under paperwork on his desk? There was no indication of the time or date of the call or even the fact that they were Iowa plates. Just the numbers and letters. Like an incomplete code. He couldn't put his finger on it, but something didn't feel right about the situation.

He locked eyes with Cal, who was lumbering toward him from across the room.

"Nice young lady, your Miss Jones." The sheriff parked his six-foot-four-inch frame in front of the desk. "Pretty, too."

Gideon sneaked a glance at Dani. She looked terrified. This was the moment to share his suspicions about Dani being set up. But before he did that, he needed to gauge the sheriff's intentions.

"What's the deal here, Cal? She looks scared out of her wits."

"I told her I was going to have to hold her for further questioning. I know that's not what you want to hear, but I don't have a choice."

"Sure you do." Frustration added an edge to his tone. "Doesn't this situation strike you as just a bit too pat? First, you get a tip about a van bringing cocaine onto the reservation, and then the Blooming Prairie police find drugs in her car. You're way too savvy to accept this stuff at face value. Think about it. What kind of person leaves cocaine on the front seat of a vehicle before delivering drugs to a reservation in North Dakota?"

"Right off the top of my head, I can think of

three." Cal Stanek took off his hat and straightened the brim in his hands. "Someone in a hurry. Someone who is so addicted she just doesn't care. Or someone who wants to make a boatload of cash and doesn't expect to get caught because she's allied herself with a group of innocent-looking kids."

"Okay. But one quick question about the initial tip regarding the van that was headed in this direction. Who took the call, and what did the person on the other end of the line say?"

"That's two questions." Cal shook his head. It didn't look like he was going to share the details, but then he shrugged as if it didn't matter. As if Dani's arrest was already a done deal. "Deputy Faegre handled the tip. Caller described the vehicle as a light blue van with Iowa plates. That's about it."

"No license number?"

"Not that I recall."

It was time to put his cards on the table. "Listen, Cal. Despite what you may think, this is no open-and-shut case. When I brought the kids in, I told you about the SUV I saw at the scene of the accident. Since then, Dani has been shot at twice and almost strangled. She's the victim here, not the mastermind of a scheme to bring drugs to the reservation."

Cal's cell buzzed, and he held a finger up as

he swiveled sideways to take the call. A moment later, he slipped the phone back into his pocket and turned to face Gideon.

"That was Deputy Faegre. The fire department wasn't able to save the barn, but it looks like the cabin is okay. I'm sorry, Gideon. This is bad business. And you seem to be caught in the middle of it." Cal glanced over at Dani and then lowered his voice. "I hear what you're saying, but try to see it from my point of view. A million dollars' worth of cocaine was hidden in a van she was driving. So, there's no possible way I can allow her to walk out of here today."

And just like that Gideon made up his mind. He knew Dani hadn't tried to bring drugs to the reservation. And after a few days of investigation, Cal would know it, too. But only if the system worked the way it was supposed to. Experience had proven that was not always the case. And with a possible dirty deputy in the mix, all bets were off.

EIGHT

A bag of cocaine had been discovered on the front seat of her car.

Dani took a deep breath and exhaled slowly as she tried to wrap her head around what the sheriff had said.

The awful implications of the latest allegations hit her like a bolt of lightning.

And even though she was now safe, there was still the possibility that she would end up in jail. If that happened, who would take care of the kids? How would they get home to Iowa? And what would their parents think when they learned that the chaperone they had trusted had been charged with trafficking twenty kilos of cocaine?

And what about her own parents? Hadn't they been through enough already? The thought of her mom and dad dealing with yet another tragedy filled her heart with pain.

Why would anyone do this? None of the answers she could come up with made sense. Except one. Could it somehow be connected with her sister's death?

Years of counseling insisted that theory was impossible. The man who killed Ali was serving a life sentence without parole. It was irrational to imagine he'd escaped from a maximum-security prison and come back to harm her. She reached up and touched the medallion she wore on a thin chain around her neck. On that flat silver disk, the words to the Serenity Prayer were inscribed in tiny script, too small for someone without a magnifying glass to read. It had been a gift from her parents on her twenty-first birthday, their not-so-subtle way of reminding her that there were things she couldn't change, no matter how hard she tried. Her eyes filled with tears, making the message even harder to read, but it didn't matter. She knew the words by heart.

God, grant me the serenity to accept the things I cannot change, the courage to change the things I can and the wisdom to know the difference.

She had learned long ago that she couldn't change the fact that her sister had died at the hands of a ruthless killer. She couldn't change the fact that she missed Ali every single day. But she could honor Ali's memory and keep it alive. And that was what she had set out to do.

Volunteering to help young teens. Majoring in science and choosing a job working with DNA. She had been determined not to squander even one minute of the time she'd been given. If she could make a difference in some small way, then it would all be worth it.

But here she was, sitting in a sheriff's office, accused of smuggling drugs. There was some consolation in the fact that Gideon finally seemed to recognize that she was innocent of the charges. Unfortunately, the sheriff didn't, and he was the one in charge.

It was disheartening, especially since the interview with Sheriff Stanek had started out well. He had tossed a few softball questions her way, leaning forward to listen as she explained that she'd never used any kind of drugs at all and that, except for what she had seen in movies, she had no idea what a kilo of cocaine even looked like.

That was when he told her about the drugs found in her car and then added in the clincher. Apparently, the cocaine in her Nissan was the same grade as the stuff in the van, a fact which the sheriff claimed to find intriguing.

Intriguing didn't seem like a good thing, especially when he followed that up with the news that he had decided to hold her for further questioning. Once he dropped that bombshell, he excused himself and went to talk to Gideon.

She looked across the room to where the two men were huddled in a whispered debate. It wasn't a stretch to assume their discussion had something to do with the cocaine.

If only she could make Sheriff Stanek understand that she was the last person in the world who would ever smuggle drugs. She had never even received a speeding ticket. Sure, she had been stopped once or twice for driving over the limit. But she had always gotten off with a stern lecture and a warning. She hadn't even been in a police station since…well, since her sister's body was found in the Dumpster and she had asked to go along with her parents to talk to the detectives who'd worked on the case.

Sheriff Stanek finished his conversation with Gideon and headed back to his desk just as his cell phone rang again. He turned sideways toward the window to take the call, frowning as he held the receiver close to his ear. Dani was so intent on studying his expression that she didn't notice Gideon had sidled up next to her. Without taking his eyes off the sheriff, he dropped a piece of paper onto the desk and then turned on his heel and walked away. She waited a moment before casting her eyes downward to read the note.

"Tell C that you need to use the ladies' room. Go out the back door to the truck and get out of here as fast as you can." At the bottom was a hastily scrawled map with directions to 322 Magnolia Lane.

She folded the paper in half and slipped it into her pocket. A chill ran up her spine as she considered the implications of what Gideon was telling her to do. He was asking her to become a fugitive.

Something desperate and immediate came through in his hurried penmanship, and she made up her mind on the spot that she would do as he asked. He had already earned her trust, and putting her faith in him seemed justified. She was tempted to take out the note and read it again, but it was fortunate that she didn't. When she looked up, the sheriff was standing beside her, looking even more somber than he had before. He mentioned something about taking her fingerprints. She pretended to listen as she plotted her escape.

In a voice that she could barely recognize as her own, she asked if there was a bathroom she could use. Cal paused for just a nanosecond and then nodded, pointing to a hallway at the back of the room.

"Thanks." She shot him an apologetic look. "I just need a few minutes, and I'll be right back."

She wanted to turn to look at Gideon for reassurance, but she kept her eyes fixed on the corridor along the hall. She needed to keep moving forward. Her heart was pounding so hard she was sure everyone could hear it. A second of hesitation, and she might give herself away. In her head, she recited the address on the note. *Three twenty-two Magnolia Lane.* The first door on the left led to the men's room; the second one, to the ladies'. Legs trembling, she walked past both and headed toward the exit in the back.

"So, how about those Grizzlies?" Gideon leaned against the side of Cal Stanek's desk, positioning his body to block the sheriff's view of the hall. "I still can't believe they've won five of their last six games. If they keep it up, they'll be sure to make it to State in March."

Cal shot him a questioning look and then shook his head with weary pessimism. "They have been doing well on the court. But their star center flipped his ATV yesterday. Broke his leg in two places, so he'll be out for the season. It's hard to say what the coach will do next, given the weakness of the bench."

The two men listened for a moment as the clock on the wall ticked away the seconds that Dani had been gone. At the same time, they both glanced down the hall toward the ladies' room door as if expecting it to open imminently.

"How about a cup of coffee?" Cal asked.

Gideon nodded and followed Cal to the counter by the back wall, where a Keurig coffee maker was set next to a basket of K-Cups.

"Medium or dark roast?"

"Dark." As Cal pushed a button on the machine, Gideon sneaked a glance at the clock. It was half past noon, which meant that Dani already had a five-minute head start.

Cal handed him a disposable foam cup and fitted a mug into the machine. He tapped his boot as he waited for the coffee to brew. An awkward silence filled the room.

"Listen, Gideon. I know you want to believe the girl isn't involved in any criminal activity. And now that I've talked with her, I'll agree that she doesn't seem the type to be mixed up in something like this. But I just can't buy into the idea that someone's trying to set her up. It just doesn't hold water, not with this much money at stake. Most drug runners wouldn't be willing to sacrifice that much revenue to ruin someone's reputation. Come back with a theory that makes more sense, and I'll be more than happy to give it a listen."

Gideon took a slow sip of coffee from his cup. He didn't want to argue with Cal, and besides, what was there to say? In the past few days, he'd kicked around the exact same thought. He had just arrived at a different conclusion.

Cal glanced down the hallway again, shaking his head. "The deputy investigating the arson ought to be back any minute, so you can talk to him when he gets here. From the sound of things, the barn is going to need a total rebuild. I guess your new boat was destroyed. That's a big loss, even worse than the barn."

"Yeah, well." He shrugged. "It is what it is." He looked down and stared at the black liquid in his cup. His boat was the least of his concerns. "Can we just talk about this for a minute, Cal? Something hasn't seemed right from the first about this case. And I think you know it, too. You're too good a cop to not recognize a frame-up as blatant as this."

Cal laughed. "There may be an insult buried in that statement, but I'm going to let it slide." His tone darkened. "Are you sure you aren't letting what happened in Miami color your judgment about this case?"

Miami? What did Cal know about that? He hadn't shared the details about what had happened with his partner with anyone outside his family, but the information was out there, just a click away. It made sense that the sheriff would be curious about why one of the town's more re-clusive citizens had left the DEA.

Cal's eyes shot toward the hallway at the sound of the back door banging open and then closed.

Gideon looked, too. Did Dani have a problem trying to start the truck and decided to sneak back inside?

A tall redhead with a half-dozen plastic gro-cery bags looped around her wrists rushed into the station. Gideon recognized her as Gina, the receptionist, and from the look of the logo on the sacks, she had just gotten back from a trip to the little grocery store on the reservation.

"Hey, Cal. I got all the stuff for the…" She no-ticed that her boss wasn't alone and reached up and patted her carefully coiffed hair. "Hi there, Gideon. I was expecting that we might be see-ing you today. I'm sorry to hear about the fire at your place. Just give me a minute to put this stuff in the refrigerator and I'll be right back."

"Say, Gina," Cal called out, "after you put those bags down, do you think you can help me out with something?"

Gina stopped halfway through the doorway and twirled around to face him. "What do you need, Boss?"

Cal glanced down the hallway. "A young woman I was interviewing went to the ladies' room about ten minutes ago. Would you go in and make sure everything's okay?"

Gideon began a silent countdown to the moment of reckoning. Cal's eyes were dark and wary. Maybe he already suspected something wasn't right.

Five, four, three, two, one. Gina popped her head out of the door.

"There's no one in here, Boss."

Cal mumbled something under his breath as he turned to glower at Gideon.

"Is your truck still in the lot?" His eyes were steely as he grabbed the keys to his cruiser and headed toward the door.

"Boss, wait!" Gina's voice stopped both men in their tracks. "On my way back to the station, I saw a green F-150 heading south toward Magnolia Lane. Did your missing witness steal Gideon's truck?"

"Thanks, Gina." Cal spoke through gritted teeth as he turned to face Gideon. "Since you currently seem to be without a vehicle, would you like to join me on a drive to the reservation? I think we both know who lives on Magnolia Lane. Abby likes to keep to herself these days, but I'm sure she'd welcome a visit from an old friend and her brother."

Neither man spoke on the five-minute drive to the reservation. The look on Cal's face was

enough to silence a caged squirrel. Battle lines
had been drawn, and Gideon had sided with
Dani.

The cruiser bumped along the potholed road,
past the local chapter of Veterans of Foreign
Wars and the small grocery store that serviced
the reservation, and entered a two-block neighborhood of wooden houses on the western shore
of the lake. By the time they pulled in front of
the neat gray bungalow, the atmosphere inside
the cruiser was almost as frosty as the air outside.

The sheriff wasted no time rocketing up the
steps, fist poised and ready to bang on the door.

Abby beat him to the punch. Clutching a teal
pashmina around her shoulders, Gideon's sister pushed open the aluminum storm door and
stepped out onto the porch.

"Cal! Great so see you! And you've brought
Gideon along, too! How nice." With her over-the-
top excitement, she managed to convey something akin to the happy coincidence of meeting
both of them unexpectedly on a tropical beach.

"Cut it out, Abby." Cal's lips turned down in
a menacing frown. "You knew we were coming.
I saw you watching by the window. Just tell me
where Dani Jones is hiding and I might forget
the fact that you're guilty of aiding and abetting
a person of interest in a criminal case."

Cal's imperious tone failed to make the woman flinch. "Who's Dani Jones? Is this some kind of joke? Are we on some police reality show where innocent people are accused of a crime to see how they react?"

Gideon leaned forward and kissed her cheek. "Hi, Abs. Sorry to bother you. Cal thinks you know something about a young woman who sneaked out of the station during an interview. She also stole my truck, so really, I'm the one who should be concerned."

Abby's amused laughter jingled in the cold air. "Maybe you should be filing a report at the station instead of complaining about it to me."

"Drop the Little Miss Innocent act, Abby." Cal was not amused. "A witness reported seeing a green F-150 heading in this direction. I know Dani Jones is here, probably in the next room, listening to this ridiculous conversation."

"Who's your witness, Cal?" Abby wanted to know. "Is it Gina? Because that girl wouldn't recognize Brad Pitt if he was standing next to her in line at the Stop 'N Shop, especially if she wasn't wearing her glasses."

Cal scowled. "Since this seems to be such a big joke to you, I assume you won't care if I take a little peek inside your garage." He pointed to the domed carport in the back of the bungalow.

"It looks just the right size to fit a truck. Mind if I check it out?"

Gideon was quick to intervene. "I'm sure Abby would be more than willing to let you search her garage, but you know as well as I do that you're going to need a warrant to do that. After all, she might have a stockpile of contraband whiskey in there, and I'd hate to see her get busted because she didn't know her rights."

Cal amped up his meanest glare. "Are you two working as a tag team here? First, Gideon distracts me so that Dani Jones can sneak out of the station, and now Abby plays dumb about hiding the truck and probably the girl."

"What?" Abby was all righteous indignation. "Why, that's the most insulting thing anyone ever said to me! You should be ashamed of yourself, Cal Stanek, for making such a vile insinuation."

For a moment, Cal was silent. But Abby's words lost much of their effect as the air was pierced with the sound of high-pitched whimpering, coming from inside the house.

The sheriff snorted. "Sounds like you have company, Abby. I'd ask if it was Lou, but I'd rather not force you to tell another lie." With an angry glare, he turned and began to walk away, his boots sliding to a halt when he was halfway down the path. "I'll be back with a warrant." He addressed his final words to Gideon. "On the off chance that you still believe in the rule of the law, you might want to suggest to Miss Jones that she turn herself in. We're her best hope for getting to the bottom of this whole ugly mess."

Abby snaked her arm around Gideon's waist as they watched the squad car disappear around the corner and out of sight.

"Thanks, sis." He gave her a solemn smile. "I owe you one."

"You owe me more than one." Abby's voice was quiet, and he wondered if she was feeling bad about lying to Cal. "One for Lou, whose leg is a mess. I'll do what I can for him, but I'm a paramedic, not a vet. Two for calming down your hysterical girlfriend when she came to the door. And three for hiding your truck, which barely made it up the driveway."

"She's not my girlfriend."

Abby raised a skeptical brow. "If you say so. But since I've never known you to break the rules…"

"She's being set up to take the fall for a crime she didn't commit."

"Just like you were in Miami."

Trust Abby to find a circular kind of logic in his quest to help Dani. "All I'm doing is trying to uncover who's behind all of this."

"A damsel in distress who appeals to your

protective instincts? Glad to hear it. I was starting to wonder if you'd ever care enough to get
involved again." She reached up and tousled his
hair. "So, you want to hear my idea for getting
the two of you out of here right under Cal's big
fat nose?"

NINE

Abby had come through for him again.

Two years ago, when he'd appeared on her doorstep a broken man, she had put her own life on hold to help him fix his. She had encouraged him to build a home from the ground up, to spend his days chopping down trees and digging the foundation for his little cabin in the woods. And while he worked, she had brought him meals and books and seedlings to plant in his garden. Even as he resisted, she had encouraged him to renew old friendships and forced him to become involved in the tribe and the community around Dagger Lake. Through the long days and restless nights, she was the one person he could count on to see past the difficulties to a better future.

And now she was about to set the leg of his dog.

He set Lou on the flannel sheet on the dining room table. So far, the shepherd had been relatively compliant. But when Abby touched the skin around the wound, he yipped with pain.

Abby bent to stroke the shepherd's neck. "Should I even ask how this happened?" Her gaze bore straight into his. But if he told her the truth, she'd blame him for leaving Lou to guard the cabin against the intruders and maybe find a couple of other reasons to hold him responsible, as well.

"Let's just say it was an accident and leave it at that."

"Humph." Clearly, she wasn't buying it.

Dani stood on the other side of the table. She hadn't said a word, though he supposed she was still shaken after spending fifteen minutes crouched in a dark damp closet in the shed. Or maybe she was upset at being assigned the role of holding Lou's head during the examination. He didn't blame her. The shepherd's eyes were clouded with apprehension as Abby prepared to disinfect the wound.

He checked the time on his phone. It had been less than twenty minutes since Cal had left, which meant they were twenty minutes closer to his inevitable return. Gideon did a quick calculation of how long it would take for the sheriff to drive back to the station, find a judge who would give him permission to search a home on Sioux land and then make his way back to Magnolia Lane with a warrant. Two hours, tops.

Abby's face was a study of concentration as she fashioned a makeshift splint out of a wooden shim. Her paramedical skills didn't translate completely to nonhuman patients, but she knew how to splint a dog's leg. As she worked, she talked quietly to Lou, reassuring him that he'd feel better soon.

She frowned when she noticed Gideon watching her. "This is temporary. The leg needs to be examined by a vet."

"I know," he said.

"I'll take him to see Dr. Wallace tomorrow. He'll set it in a permanent cast and give Lou a tetanus shot if he needs one." Her eyes darted toward the door. "You two better get out of here before Cal comes back with a warrant."

Gideon looked at Dani. Anxiety lingered in her eyes. Clearly, she was worried about Lou. And maybe she was troubled by the fact that she hadn't been able to communicate with the kids in her mission group or find out how they were faring at the reservation.

But there was something else there, too.

Wariness and concern about what lay ahead.

He sidled up next to his sister and spoke in a quiet voice. "Do you still have keys to Kenny's house? Cal won't have a warrant to search his place, so we can hole up there and use the computer until he gets home from work."

Abby reached for the small pair of scissors she'd set on the table and snipped off a loose piece of tape. "Maybe you should let the sheriff handle this instead of trying to figure out everything on your own. Cal can be gruff, but he's good at his job. I'm sure he won't let Dani come to any harm."

"This whole thing is a lot more complicated than you know. I need to do it my way. Please."

Abby walked over to a desk in the corner of the room and opened a drawer. She palmed a small keychain with a large metal clip dangling from one of the sides and set it on the table next to Lou's head. "Kenny gets home at five, so you need to be out of his house by then. The only reason he trusts me with his keys is so that I can feed his cat. My laptop is in a bag by the door. Take my cell charger, too, just in case. Just don't touch anything that belongs to Kenny."

"Five o'clock," Gideon repeated, glancing at his phone. "That means I'll have a little more than three hours to find what I'm looking for."

The sour taste of regret stuck in Dani's throat as she followed Gideon down the rocky path leading from Abby's house to the neighbor's back porch. She felt more vulnerable here than she had in town. Sheriff Stanek had the law on his side. And by running away, she had relinquished that protection.

A brisk breeze slapped her hair against her cheeks and made her eyes sting from the cold. Two feet ahead, Gideon kept his head low as he climbed the wooden stairs to the porch and fitted the key into the lock. It stuck at first and then swung open to a tiny kitchen with a black-and-white-checkered linoleum floor and a sink full of dishes waiting to be washed.

Gideon pulled the door closed behind them, shrugged off his jacket and tossed it onto the counter next to the stove.

"Make yourself at home." He lifted Abby's laptop out of the bag and opened it in front of him.

Home? Her fingers trembled as she unbuttoned her coat. Home was five hundred miles away in Blooming Prairie, not here, in a stranger's house in Dagger Lake.

She added breaking and entering to the growing list of charges that could be leveled against her. Maybe the fact that Gideon used a key to gain entry to Kenny's house made their current crime less of an issue. Not that it mattered at the moment. In any case, Gideon stood to lose almost as much as she did if they were caught. He had put his own reputation on the line to help her escape.

Gideon bent to plug in the charger for his phone. When the red light went on, he tilted the screen of Abby's laptop for Dani to see.

"How many people do you know who have a picture of an ambulance as a screen saver?"

She forced a smile. A pang of jealousy tugged at her heart, but she tamped it down. It was selfish to resent the fact that Gideon had a serious girlfriend. Abby had taken a big risk by helping her hide from the sheriff. She'd given Gideon her computer and phone charger and even insisted on lending Dani a pair of winter boots. And, if that wasn't enough, she had even handed them a sack of food on their way out the door.

Yup. Abby was awesome. Beautiful. Kind. Thoughtful. The perfect match for a man like Gideon. Except… Dani shook off her unworthy thoughts and asked herself why the idea of Abby and Gideon caused her so much distress. As she had said more than once, she wasn't looking for a relationship. Especially now. And especially not with a man like Gideon. He was far too set in his ways, with his solitary life in his isolated cabin. Besides, she had enough on her plate at the moment. She'd be happy to survive another day and escape from the men who were trying to kill her.

And even if the thugs were caught, the case solved and her reputation restored, she wouldn't be ready for a relationship. Hadn't her boss at work hinted at the possibility of a promotion? That would mean extra hours on the job and less time for leisure since she wasn't about to give up any of the time she spent volunteering with the kids. Not only that, but her folks were getting older. As their only surviving child, she knew that all the responsibility for their well-being fell squarely on her shoulders.

Gideon reached into the bag and pulled out a couple of sandwiches, two bottles of juice and a Tupperware container of cookies and set them in the middle of the table.

"Help yourself." He picked up a sandwich and held it in one hand as he tapped on the keyboard. "I was thinking that we should begin by focusing on your job. What's the name of the place you work?"

"Danford." She leaned forward to look as the familiar yellow-and-green logo popped up on the screen. "'Danford Labs. DNA Testing—Confidential Answers Quickly.'" She read aloud.

In a nutshell, those were the two things most of their clients wanted—privacy and speedy results. "There's nothing on the website about our clients. That information is confidential. Even the police departments that use us to process crime scene DNA don't want their names out there for the public to see."

"So when you perform a test, you aren't aware of the identity of the person who provided the sample?"

"No. My supervisor is the only one with that information, and she keeps all those files on her computer." She selected a cookie from the container on the table and nibbled around the edges. Oatmeal, chewy with plenty of raisins. Was there anything Abby couldn't do perfectly?

Gideon scratched his head. "There has to be another way to get that information. I'm going to start by checking criminal cases on the docket and see where we can go from there."

Dani wound her hands around her bottle of orange juice, feeling useless as Gideon shifted his eyes back to the keyboard. "What are you looking for?"

"A trial involving DNA." He blew out a sigh as he counted the possibilities on his fingers. "A defendant wealthy enough to spend a million dollars to make a problem disappear. And someone desperate enough to eliminate anyone standing in the way."

"But at this point, no one can change the results of the test. The evidence has been recorded. It's a done deal."

Gideon's eyes flashed with canny intelligence.

"That's true. But imagine how it would affect your reputation if you were indicted for drug smuggling. Those kinds of charges would go a long way toward discrediting your testimony in court, assuming you live long enough to make it that far."

What Gideon was saying made sense. Until two days ago, her integrity had been beyond reproach. She was recognized for her thoroughness and accuracy, but the men who'd planted the cocaine aimed to change all of that. They had set things up to make her look like someone who trafficked drugs. Someone who was careless enough to botch a test while under the influence.

It had taken years of hard work to build her reputation and less than two days to tear it down. When she got the job at Danford, she had dedicated her life to solving crimes like the one against Ali. But now, thanks to someone with a vendetta against her, there was a good chance it would all be in vain.

Her mind reeled with the futility of it all. If only there was some other way to explain the smuggled cocaine. Her thoughts wound back to the person who had haunted her for fifteen years. Ali's murderer.

"I understand what you're saying about my job being a logical reason for someone wanting to set me up. But what about the man who killed my sister, Ali? Have you ruled him out as a suspect? I know he's supposed to be in jail, but what if he's not? He always threatened to come after me. As he was escorted out of court on the last day of the trial, he pointed and me and said, 'Better watch your back, little girl. I'm coming for you next.'"

Gideon stopped typing. He clenched a muscle in his jaw as he pushed aside the computer and met her glance. "Okay. Let's see what I can find out about this guy. What was his name again?"

It hurt her ears to speak his name. "Richard Monroe."

"Do you remember where he was incarcerated?"

She shook her head.

Gideon picked up his phone and tapped in a number. "Hey, Tom. How are you?... Right... Right... I know... Absolutely... It has been a while. Listen, I wonder if you could check on someone for me. Felon by the name of Richard Monroe. Victim was a thirteen-year-old girl named Ali Jones... Sure. Take all the time you need."

He cradled the phone against his shoulder and twirled his pencil as he waited for his contact to come back on the line.

"Thanks, man. I owe you one." He hung up

and plugged his phone into the charger. His eyes softened as they fixed on hers. "According to roll call this morning, Monroe is still serving a life sentence at the Menard Correctional Center in Southern Illinois. He's not getting around too well these days because of a broken leg. Apparently, there was some sort of accident in the lunchroom."

Dani opened her mouth to speak but instead took a large gulp of air. She blinked away a picture of Richard Monroe in his tiny cell, a large plaster cast on his leg. Though she had seen him every day at the trial, she barely remembered what he looked like. Over the years, she had constructed an image of a monster, large and invincible, with strong arms and evil, hooded eyes. Now, all of a sudden, she had to update that memory to include an aging face and a broken leg. And to accept the fact that Richard Monroe wasn't the one responsible for setting her up.

"I'm sorry you had to go through so much trouble to put my mind at ease." She forced a sad smile.

Gideon shook his head. "No trouble at all. The first rule of a good investigator is to follow every lead."

He was being kind. Right off the bat, he had understood the improbability of a man like Richard Monroe having the resources to purchase and plant that much cocaine. But rather than discount her fears or ignore her suspicions, he'd made the necessary inquiries and treated her with respect. It was a glimpse of the kind of DEA agent Gideon must have been. Thoughtful. Considerate. Caring. A rush of emotion deeper than any that she had ever felt tugged at her core. But she couldn't let Gideon see what she was feeling. He had already been dragged too deep into the black hole of her problems. She had to hide the tenderness surging into her heart.

"So, what's next?" Her eyes fixed on the computer, where the Danford logo was still flashing on the screen. "What can I do to help?"

"It's almost three o'clock. I still need to make a few more calls, so maybe you should take a nap while you have the chance." He tilted his head toward the adjoining room. "Go stretch out on the couch. I'll wake you when it's time to go."

The past few nights had been brutal, and her brain was barely functioning for lack of sleep. A two-hour catnap would go a long way in restoring her peace of mind. But Gideon had to be more exhausted than she was. He was the one who needed to catch some shut-eye.

She pointed at the couch. "Why don't you go lie down, and I'll see what I can find on the computer? Sometimes a set of fresh eyes can see things that get missed." It was a lame suggestion, and she knew it.

He shook his head. "I'm too wired to sleep. I need to make a few calls. You go. Please."

"Okay." So much for good intentions. She hated to give up that easily, but she felt her legs pushing back from her chair and leading her into the living room.

The tan microfiber sofa felt like velvet as she stretched out on the cushions, her hand cupping the side of her head. In the background, Gideon's voice rose and fell in a lulling tempo as he talked on the phone in the kitchen. She caught a word here and there—*cocaine, DNA, trial*— but his murmurings served only as white noise to keep the nightmares at bay.

The rat-a-tat of a fist pounding against wood woke her with a start.

How long had she been sleeping? Was the sound part of a dream, or was someone knocking at the door? A surge of adrenaline left her heart pounding rapidly in her chest. Gideon stood with his back to the wall, his fingers cracking the edge of one of the blinds to form a slit wide enough to peek through.

"It's Cal," Gideon whispered. "He's probably checking the homes in the neighborhood and asking if anyone has seen anything unusual."

The banging picked up in intensity, almost

like the sheriff was trying to hammer a hole in the door. Panic gripped her throat. She could hardly hear her voice as she breathed her response. "What should we do?"

"If we don't answer, he'll move on. At least, I hope he will."

Her eyes locked on Gideon. He was putting his reputation on the line to help her, and her heart swelled with gratitude. And the stirring of something more. A hope. A wish. An unfulfilled dream. The feelings surged and then slipped like water through her hands as she forced a reality check. She was alive, and Ali was dead. Why would she ever think she deserved more?

Fifteen years hadn't erased the shame that she was the one spared that awful day. Her counselor had diagnosed the problem in two words. *Survivor's guilt.* The feeling that she should have been the one taken, not Ali. But her counselor didn't understand. No one did. It wasn't guilt fueling her actions. It was a desire to keep her world in balance and to prove that Ali's death had not been in vain.

The banging stopped. Gideon waited for a moment before he peered out the window.

"He's gone. We need to leave here soon, anyway. Abby phoned a few minutes ago to say that she got called in to work. Apparently, she talked a friend of hers into lending us a car. He's at a wedding at the VFW, so we'll stop there first to get the keys. I need three minutes to gather up my gear, and then we'll go out the way we came in. The VFW is less than a mile from here, but the way the wind is blowing, it's going to be cold."

Her mind reeled. A wedding? The VFW? What exactly was the plan?

TEN

They ran as if someone was chasing them, but no one was, at least as far as he could see. With their heads down, they sprinted through the backyard, out the gate and between the houses toward the woods.

The Dagger Lake reservation comprised more than thirty-two thousand acres of pine forest and rugged farmland that extended beyond the county line. Two blocks north of Magnolia Lane, there was a wooded area with lots of cover. If they could make it there without being seen, the trees would offer shelter from the sheriff's prying eyes.

Gideon had the stamina to maintain the pace for miles, but Dani was struggling. Her face was ashen, and she was clutching her arms to her side. He shortened his stride as they approached the fence on the edge of the woods. Pushing aside the wire, he let Dani duck under and then followed behind.

"You okay?" He turned to face her. She was leaning against a pine tree, gulping air.

"Fine."

He must have looked like he didn't believe her, because she straightened and exhaled sharply.

"Really. I'm good. Let's keep going."

"Okay. But maybe we should take it easy for a while."

For the second time in as many minutes, she shot him a look. He needed to work harder on maintaining his game face. Cool, calm and collected. That was the ticket. But it was difficult to do, knowing that the sheriff was on the prowl and that the thugs had shotguns. And probably high-powered rifles, as well.

"Gideon?" Dani touched his arm. Her voice shook with uncertainty. "Do you think someone is following us?"

"I'm not sure. But if they are, we have the advantage. I know these woods like the back of my hand. Abby and I used to play here when we were little."

"Abby?" Dani tripped on a tree root and stumbled to the ground.

He offered her a hand up. Holding on to his arm, she brushed a smattering of brown pine needles off her coat. She looked so... He struggled to think of a word to describe the expression on her face. *Forlorn? Disappointed?* It wasn't surprising. The entire day had been an ordeal from start to finish. It took a force of will not to reach out and hug her to his chest.

"Yeah. For years, all she did was follow me around." There was a picture somewhere of two-year-old Abby holding him at the hospital right after he was born. According to family lore, she had set up a sleeping bag next to his crib. And when he was finally old enough to go to school, she had walked him to kindergarten every morning and waited for him outside his classroom door at the end of the day.

"That must have been fun." Dani's voice brought him back to reality.

More like annoying, but he wouldn't complain. He had definitely done well in the big-sister department.

Dani bent to pick up a branch on the path and tossed it into the brush. "Did you come upon anything interesting in your internet search?"

"I found some stuff that might pan out. There's a big case set to go to trial this week in Des Moines. A state senator, accused of the hit-and-run death of a Cambodian immigrant. You know anything about that?"

She shook her head.

"How about the name Patrick Ravelli? Does that ring any bells?"

"Sorry. I don't usually watch the news or read

the paper. I should, I know. But work has been crazy, and with all of my church group duties, I never find the time."

"I'm just as bad." He shrugged. "No news is good news, I always say."

She smiled at him.

"Anyway." He struggled to stay on point. The last thing he needed was to start making decisions based on a smile that did funny things to his heart. Best to stick to the facts and keep his emotions at bay. "The police claim to have a solid case against Ravelli, but his lawyers are denying he was anywhere near the scene. The initial reports didn't mention anything about DNA, but there was a hint about recently discovered evidence that will rock the case at trial. We'll see what turns up. I left a couple of messages for my buddy at the DOJ." He patted the cell phone in his pocket. "I'm waiting to hear what he has to say."

"Do you think this Patrick Ravelli could be the person who planted the drugs?"

"I'm not sure about anything yet." The last thing he wanted to do was raise her hopes, only to have them dashed if his theory didn't hold. *Don't make promises you can't keep.* The vow he had made two years ago echoed in his mind. They needed to take things one step at a time. "First, I need to confirm that there is a DNA component to this case. If there is, I'll make a few more calls and see if I can find a connection to Danford Labs."

Dani looked over at him, her eyes filling with tears. "I don't know what I'd do without your help, Gideon. I'm so thankful to God for sending you into my life."

"Not a problem." His voice was cool and detached, but his insides were churning with frustration. Remaining emotionally uninvolved was proving more and more difficult. He felt unbridled fury at the men who had caused Dani this much distress. She had been through a lot already, coping with the loss of her sister and the threats on her own life. But she hadn't let any of it get her down. She had turned her sorrow into positive energy. And, unlike him, she had never lost faith in the mercy of God.

In the distance, a dog howled. Dani stopped short.

"Do you think Lou will be okay?"

He took a deep breath. "I do. Abby will get him to the vet tomorrow to look at that leg. Knowing her, she'll bring him home and spoil him rotten." He pointed to a clearing in the woods ahead. "We're almost there. The VFW is at the end of the block."

Dani wiped her eyes with the back of her mitten. "I need to stop getting so worked up about everything. After all, we've made it this far without getting arrested or shot."

That seemed to be setting the bar pretty low. If Dani got arrested or shot, it would mean that he had failed. Only complete exoneration from the drug charges and restoration of her reputation were acceptable outcomes to the mission. In his line of work, he had seen plenty of people haunted by bad choices, but Dani wasn't one of them. She was an innocent, caught in the crossfire of events they had only begun to understand. She was the type of woman he could fall for, given half a chance. But she deserved better than a man with a wounded and bitter heart.

A fallen tree blocked the path to the clearing. He extended his hand to help Dani climb over it.

"Gideon?" She was doing that lip-biting thing again. If the situation wasn't so dire, he might think it was cute. He needed to keep his focus. "I'm sorry you had to get involved in this. It's bad enough that someone is trying to frame me. But now you're implicated, as well."

"I want to help you. Those criminals who set my barn on fire and stabbed my dog made this personal for me, as well. This is all going to be over soon, Dani. Once I get the keys to Abby's friend's car, I can get you out of here and then see what I can do about solving this case."

That was the plan, at least. Whether or not

the execution would go off without a hitch remained to be seen.

Dani furrowed her brow. "This wedding we're crashing? I know it's too cold to wait outside, but my clothes are too casual for such a solemn occasion."

He hadn't stopped to consider their attire. His eyes did a quick once-over of her appearance. White coat. A bit dirty in places, but they'd check it at the door. Boots. It was winter. That's what everyone wore around here. Jeans. Well, they were a bit informal, but no one would care.

"You look fine," he said. That was the understatement of the year. Her cheeks were pink and glowing, and curls of hair had escaped her cap in soft tendrils around her face.

She was beautiful. But no way was he going to tell her that. He was already in too deep. His heart and his brain were on a dangerous collision course, and experience had taught him that emotions had no place in an investigation. Scratch that. Emotions had no place in his life.

She slowed her pace. "We'll only need to stay at the reception for a few minutes, right?"

"Just long enough for me to find Pete and get his keys."

And he still needed to talk with his buddy at the Department of Justice. If his theory about the DNA evidence didn't pan out, it would be back to square one, making calls and searching for leads on the computer. But at this point, why look for reasons to stress?

The pines thinned out and the ground crackled under a dusting of snow. Just like that, they were in the open, jogging down the shoulder of a busy street. His eyes darted left and right, checking out the landscape. A dozen cars and trucks were parked along the curb, but there didn't appear to be any active police presence in the vicinity. That was a relief. The last thing he needed was to walk into the hall and run into Sheriff Cal Stanek.

They crossed the street and walked down a path scraped clean of snow that led to the one-story building housing the local chapter of VFW. A lot of people never thought about it, but there were plenty of men and women from these parts who had served their country abroad—Afghanistan, Iraq, Korea, Vietnam and even a few who had fought in World War II. The place itself was nothing fancy, but it was a popular venue for special events. He didn't know the happy couple who had just gotten married, but from the number of vehicles in the lot and on the street, they had invited half the town.

As he pushed open the broad front door of the

building, the enticing aroma of sizzling meat assailed his nostrils. Steak! His stomach growled at the prospect of cutting into a juicy ribeye.

Dani followed him over to the coat check, where he slid his tan parka across the counter and waited as the girl behind the Dutch doors clipped a ticket to the collar.

"Shall I put your friend's stuff with yours?" The coat check girl was short and dark-skinned, with a thin band of freckles across her nose. He probably knew her folks from tribal councils that Abby forced him to attend. He didn't really mind, though he pretended to, just to give her a hard time. At some point, he needed to take her advice and get more involved in the community.

Dani shrugged off her coat and set it on the counter. "My jeans are covered in pine needles and ripped at the knee. Are you really sure this is okay?"

"People around here don't dress up for weddings." He pocketed the claim check, took her arm and piloted her toward the large double doors of the banquet room. "We're not like city folk, who get all decked out in fancy clothes just to stand around and watch a couple get hitched. Around here, people know how to throw a party."

He kept his tone light and his smile fixed to

disguise his growing concern that a fresh set of problems awaited them behind those closed doors.

Dani prepared for the moment of reckoning as Gideon pushed open the doors to the banquet hall. It was impossible not to be self-conscious about the way she was dressed. Not to mention the fact that neither one of them had actually been invited to the reception.

The last wedding she'd attended had been a posh affair at the country club, with tuxedoed waiters and a classical quartet. But despite the gourmet food and the beautiful setting, no one— not even the bride and groom—appeared to be having fun.

But Gideon was right. This looked like a party. A seven-piece country band had set up at one end of the hall. The lead singer, in a wide-brimmed cowboy hat and a pair of pressed jeans, was belting out an oldie by George Strait, and the dance floor was packed. She slowed her pace to watch, but Gideon's fingers pressed against her elbow, guiding her toward a round table on the far side of the room.

"Bob, Carrie, Tammy, Cole, Linda, Pete." Gideon moved a finger clockwise as he recited the names of the men and women seated in a circle. Apparently, few people in Dagger Lake had gotten the memo about not dressing up. This group was wearing their Sunday best. Gideon tilted his head sideways toward her. "This is Dani Jones."

"Well, hey there, Gideon. I didn't know you were invited to this shindig." The woman Gideon had identified as Linda raised a curious brow.

"I wasn't. I'm here to talk to Pete about his car."

Pete, a heavyset man with a wide smile, pushed back his chair. He bent to say something to the woman beside him before ambling over to stand next to Gideon.

Gideon tossed his arm over her shoulders as he leaned in to speak to Pete. The pressure of his fingertips on her arm caused a blush of heat to slowly creep up her throat. As the two men talked, she let her eyes scan the room. By most standards, the hall was large, with about forty tables in a semicircle in front of the dance floor. The servers were hustling to clear plates and re-fill pitchers of water as the band took a break between sets.

Pete reached into his pocket and pulled out a key. He muttered something about the air conditioner not working, and Gideon laughed and said it wouldn't be an issue.

Gideon's arm felt nice around her shoulder, but Dani considered changing her position to make some room between them. It wouldn't do to have the guests in the room think that... What would they think, exactly? Gideon had a girlfriend. Abby. And she didn't want these strangers wondering why he was getting cozy with her while his steady girl was nowhere in sight.

Someone tapped the side of a glass champagne flute, and the room grew quiet as everyone turned toward the main table to await a speech from the father of the bride. Beside her, Gideon shifted his weight from one leg to the next, no doubt anxious to be on their way.

"We'll leave as soon as he finishes his toast," he whispered in her ear. A slim man with a gray goatee stepped in front of the mike. He glanced at his daughter, pride and love shining in his eyes for all to see. He said a few words about the joys of fatherhood in a speech that earned him a hug around the neck from the bride. After a few minutes, the band struck up a slow song, and Pete slipped away to rejoin his friends.

Gideon shifted his arm from Dani's shoulders to hook it around her waist. The warm glow of a few minutes earlier turned into a heated flush as they began to sway to the music. "I'm going to dance us across the floor," he said in a low voice. "When no one's looking, we'll slip out the door. At least that's the plan at the moment."

A plan. She sighed at the thought of something so ordered and logical. After the last couple of days, the very idea seemed like a foreign concept.

She closed her eyes and allowed herself to be caught in the moment, their bodies swaying to the music and her cheek pressed against the soft flannel of Gideon's shirt. It was comforting to feel the steady beat of his heart and the weight of his arms around her waist. Gideon was a good dancer, and despite the clunky boots on her feet, it was easy to follow his lead. As they moved closer to the exit, stepping in time with the music, she had a strange realization. Even as she was she being pursued by the police and two ruthless killers, she felt happier than she had in a long time. For years, she had looked for satisfaction in her work at the lab and her volunteer activities at the church. But she finally knew what she was missing. These feelings of security and companionship. Being cherished and protected. The chance of marriage and of one day having children of her own. Yes, she wanted all that—but not now. There was too much work to do before she could dream of a different future. DNA research was opening up new leads every day, and she needed to stay the course for her sake—and for Ali's.

As the band picked up tempo, someone bumped into her side.

She opened her eyes. A short red-haired man in a navy suit stood there.

Gideon loosened his grip on her waist. "Hey, Billy," he said.

"Sorry to interrupt, but Reg has something he wants to give you." The man tilted his head toward a table on the other side of the room. "I'd be happy to dance with your girl while you're gone."

Gideon's eyes searched hers. "Do you mind?"

His question made her heart thump even faster in her chest. "No," she said, though she didn't want to change partners. She wanted to hold on to the moment as long as she could. "Go see what your friend has to say."

As Gideon walked across the hall, she placed her hand on Billy's shoulder and began to dance. They had hardly made it once around the floor when a gruff voice interrupted with a snarl.

"Mind if I cut in?"

The interloper's face was turned toward Billy, but there was something familiar in his profile. A flash of panic rose through her body as Billy stepped aside and allowed the man to take his place.

Tight arms wound around her waist as her

partner stared down at her, displeasure twisting his smile into a sinister gloat.

"Did you really think I was going to let you get away?"

ELEVEN

Trouble.

Gideon's eyes flashed on the scene twenty yards from the spot where he was standing. One minute, Dani was dancing with Billy. The next, she was being pulled toward the exit by the thug from the SUV.

Watching the brute's large fingers clamp around her waist was enough to make his blood boil. Dani seemed to be offering little resistance as her adversary locked her into a deadly dance. What had he done to secure her compliance? Had he told her he was armed and prepared to fire into the crowd if she refused to surrender to his iron grip?

Gideon fingered the two keys in his pocket: the long flat one to Pete's Crown Vic and the smaller one he had acquired just moments ago.

If you need a place to hide, even for a short time, my icehouse is just a quick ride out on the lake, Reg had said as he pressed the key to his snowmobile into Gideon's hand. *The combination on the door is 12-24-12. I keep my gun in a box under the bunk.*

Reg's gun—any gun, in fact—would come in handy just about now, though pulling a weapon in such close quarters would be a mistake. First rule of engagement: never put innocent civilians in the line of fire.

Without a weapon, he'd have to make do with his fists. He flexed his fingers in anticipation. With stealth and precision, he threaded his way through the crowded dance floor, keeping a low profile so as not to arouse his adversary's suspicion. His tactical skills came flooding back to him as his eyes scanned the room, picking up details and filing them away.

There were three exits leading to the foyer and, from there, just one set of double doors that opened to the outside.

The wedding party was posing for pictures in front of one exit. Best avoid that route if at all possible. The thug seemed headed toward the door on the right. Two-stepping in time to the music, the man pulled Dani along, his arms locked around her waist as they mingled with the other dancers. Gideon needed to stop them before they reached the exit, and do so without causing a major incident. As he moved through the crowd, his eyes trained on Dani, his senses took in the scene around him. The faint smell of beeswax as the old-fashioned candles, set in bunches of three on each of the tables, perfumed the air. The gentle drone of heat being blown through the vents. The indistinct chatter of conversations taking place all around him. The pastel tablecloths and brightly colored clothing of the wedding guests. He spotted a few old friends, but there was no time to pause and greet them. His mind registered all the peripheral data while his brain worked in overdrive to plan his next move. He calculated the seconds before the thug reached the door. Fifteen, maybe twenty, at most.

He picked up his pace, edging through the swirling dancers and keeping his head low to avoid being spotted in the crowd. The band was playing a country classic from the nineties, and the dance floor was packed with older couples and kids.

The brute must have sensed Gideon's presence because he began to pull Dani toward the door. His partner—the passenger Gideon had spotted in the tan SUV—materialized in front of the exit and stood waiting to assist. So it was two against one on a crowded dance floor. Urgency mingled with despair. There was no way to cover the distance in time to save Dani.

And then, seemingly out of nowhere, a tall

man with crisp gray hair combed up in a peak stepped between the thugs and seized the SUV driver's wrist, pumping his hand in an energetic handshake.

Mayor Steve Hovland. A man as smooth as he was charming. His aw-shucks, down-home, good-ole-boy routine was genuine, but no less deliberate as he glad-handed the crowd. Beside him stood Pete, and from the mayor's grip on the thug's hand and the glint in Pete's eyes, Gideon could only assume that this little meet and greet had not happened by accident. Best of all, the mayor was carrying. A classic Smith & Wesson revolver was strapped to the holster slung around his waist. He and Pete must have noticed what was happening and decided to intervene. The thought was almost heartwarming. If he were a sentimental sort of guy. Which he wasn't.

"Mayor. Pete." Gideon was surprised by the hitch in his voice as he joined the group. He slung a proprietary arm around Dani's shoulders and pulled her close. The thug's eyes flashed in anger as he released his grip on Dani. At the sight of the bruise forming on Dani's arm, it took all of Gideon's self-control not to throw a punch. "If you don't mind, I'd like to grab my date and enjoy another dance."

"I can't say I blame you." The mayor chuckled. "But, Gideon, it's been way too long since you and I caught up on the news. Stop by the office for a chat and a cup of coffee next week when you get the chance."

"Sure thing, sir." Gideon was smart enough to recognize an order when he heard one. Mayor Hovland might be willing to help him out this one time, but he would expect a full explanation with all the details.

"And bring that sister of yours along with you. I tell everyone who asks that Abby Marshall is the best paramedic in all of Dagger Lake. I owe her a big thank-you for performing the Heimlich on my grandson last month when he choked on an ice-cream cone at the creamery."

"Will do. C'mon, Dani. Let's show them our moves. I'll catch up with all of you later when they cut the cake."

Gideon stepped to the side as the mayor began to recount the story of that fateful day at the creamery. The two thugs squirmed uncomfortably, displeased to be a captive audience for the mayor's rambling diatribe.

Gideon wrapped his arms around Dani. "You okay?" He knew the answer. She was far from okay. She understood as he did that the men who tried to kill her were less than twenty feet away.

"They followed me from the sheriff's office." Dani's voice trembled close to his ear. "The guy who grabbed me on the dance floor said they weren't being paid to allow me to get away."

"Let's get out of here now." Gideon tightened his hold on her shoulders as he pushed open a door marked Employees Only and led her inside.

After the whir of music and muted conversation in the banquet hall, the hustle and clamor of the kitchen was jarring. Reggae music was blaring from a stereo above the stove, and cooks shouted orders across the long countertops. Dani followed Gideon past rows of shelves overflowing with boxes of food and pots and pans. A few workers shot them curious looks, but no one tried to stop them. Gideon reached into his pocket and pulled out a couple of fifty-dollar bills and the claim tickets for their coats and laid them on the counter.

"Anyone want to lend us their jackets? You can have the ones we left at coat check, and I'll return yours by the end of the week."

A cook on the line pointed to a tan parka hanging behind the door. One of the servers stepped into the closet and returned with a short purple coat.

"Thanks." He scooped them up and led Dani to a small alcove by the door. The men had probably seen them duck through the service entrance, so the sooner they got out of here the better. Sliding one arm through a sleeve of the parka, he pushed open the side door and pulled it closed in one quick motion. Two police cars were parked in the lot next to Pete's Crown Vic.

"Change of plans. We'll go through the basement and head toward the lake. Reg's snowmobile will get us to his icehouse, and we'll figure out our next steps from there."

Dani's face registered confusion, but there was no time to explain. They needed to lie low for a while, at least until the police left the scene.

He led her down a narrow staircase and through the basement to a door on the other side of the building. He cracked it open and scanned the dark lot. All clear. At least for the moment. He tossed an arm across her shoulder and walked to the path through the trees to the lakeshore.

"I didn't know," Dani whispered.

"Know what?"

"I didn't know Abby was your sister."

Really? "Sorry. In in all the excitement, I didn't make a formal introduction. Although, she would probably be happy that you didn't pick up on any family resemblance. Who did you think she was?"

"Your girlfriend."

"My girlfriend?" Huh. That she was confused on this point mystified him. But this was hardly the time to discuss such an awkward misunderstanding. "Well, it doesn't matter either way. We just need to stay low until we find Reg's snowmobile."

Dani's face registered hurt. "I'm sure you're in a hurry to get this case solved. After everything that just happened, you're probably anxious to be done with me and my problems as soon as possible."

He shot her a confused look. What was she talking about? They were being pursued by the police, not to mention ruthless criminals who had already made numerous attempts on her life, and she was acting like she wanted to stop and discuss his relationship status. And why was she behaving more reserved now that she knew he didn't have a girlfriend? Shouldn't it be the opposite?

Unless he had misunderstood her feelings toward him. The thought felt like a punch in the gut, but he quickly banished it from his head. Why did he even care?

That was the crux of the matter.

He didn't want to care. Didn't want to get emotionally involved. More important, he wasn't about to break those promises he had made to himself two years ago. Not to let his guard down. Not to trust. Falling in love was a lose-lose situation. And it was one he was determined to avoid at all costs.

TWELVE

Gideon climbed on board the snowmobile and opened the choke. "Ready to go?"

Dani gripped the side handles. "Ready as I'll ever be."

Having never ridden a snowmobile before, she was more than a little bit nervous, especially after bumping off the two-foot drop onto the lake. Adding to the fear factor, the vehicle was shaped like a large green bug, with pincers in the form of giant skis. And it had an engine that sounded like a chain saw set to full throttle.

Maybe she would be better served keeping her imagination in check. She leaned her head against the back of Gideon's parka as he steered toward the cluster of houses on the far side of the lake. It was a glorious evening. The sun had already set, but the sky was gray and laced with stringy clouds that merged into the wind-sculpted drifts along the horizon.

It was cold. In the last half hour, a chill had cut

into her bones so deep that her fingers and toes seemed permanently clenched, and her legs felt like they had frozen into two solid blocks of ice. To stop herself from obsessing about the subzero temperatures and the men in the tan SUV, she played with Gideon's words in her head.

It doesn't matter either way.

How could it not matter that Abby was Gideon's sister? It was like adjusting the sights on a pair of binoculars. All of a sudden, so many things were clear. How had she not seen it sooner? The siblings had the same dark intelligent eyes and the same oval shape to their faces. The same thoughtful expressions. The same wide but reluctant smiles.

Abby wasn't Gideon's girlfriend. But the roller coaster of emotions over the past few days had been draining, and she needed to get her heart back to a more sensible place. Sometime in the last forty-eight hours, she had stopped thinking of Gideon as a kind stranger and allowed herself to imagine the possibilities of something more. But that was a mistake. In a drawer in her dresser back at her apartment was a list of her future goals and her five-year plan on how to accomplish them. There was the promised promotion at work, which would necessitate her going back to school to get her master's degree. And she had promised to chaperone the teens' next trip to Appalachia. She had more than enough on her plate already. There wasn't room for a relationship.

Gideon's arm tensed as he engaged the brake, and she could feel the snowmobile slowing down. In front of them, outlined against the darkening sky, was an eight-by-eight-foot ice-house with a large balsam wreath on a red door.

As soon as they climbed off the vehicle and Gideon keyed in the combination to the lock, they stepped inside. A sliver of moonlight illuminated the inside of the shack in a silvery glow. Gideon fumbled for a flashlight on a shelf on the wall, then flicked it on. In the dim light, he looked like a wild man. His hair had come loose from the binder that had kept it off his face, and long dark curls hung around his eyes. The beam of the flashlight dipped across the room, coming to rest on a coffee can on a shelf above an old Coleman stove. Gideon reached inside and pulled out some matches, which he used to light a pair of kerosene lamps.

The house itself was bigger than a closet, but smaller than a one-car garage. Against one wall, there was a potbellied stove with a crate full of wood set next to it on the floor. At the other end of the room, a built-in bunk shared space with a folding table and a couple of chairs. There was a square wooden plank in the center of the floor, presumably covering the ice-fishing hole that was the reason for the entire production.

Gideon pulled off his gloves and opened his phone. She could see over his shoulder that the screen was blank. He blew on his fingers, which were white from the cold.

Five seconds ticked by as he stared at his cell. Then he tossed it aside and picked up the matches again. His hands shook as he struck a light and held it inside the stove. The spark caught the tinder and leaped in a flame.

Dani rubbed her hands together, trying to regain some circulation. "What happens now?"

He tossed a handful of wood into the stove, avoiding her eyes. "Worst comes to worst, I can catch us some fish."

She followed his gaze to the half-dozen spears stacked against the wall.

"Don't you need a rod and bait to do that?"

"Sure. But Reg's got the place equipped for dark house spearfishing. Some people around here think it should be illegal." He shrugged. "I try not to get involved in the debate."

Frustration was woven into the corners of his mouth as he surreptitiously rechecked his phone. "When this is over, I'm going to have to find a way to thank those guys for helping us. Especially Reg. He doesn't like to lend his snowmobile to anyone."

"Are all of the men you were talking to at the wedding members of the tribe?"

"Except for Pete. He works with Abby."

Abby. Since he brought the subject up, this might be her cue to address their misunderstanding.

Gideon was obviously thinking the same thing. "It's kind of funny that you didn't know Abby was my sister. But I guess I did send you off to Magnolia Lane without much information."

An awkward silence stretched between them.

"Well," she said, "it all worked out in the end. And Abby sure is nice."

"She's the best. She's the one who keeps up with all the relatives and remembers everyone's birthdays and important events. Since coming home, I haven't exactly been the most sociable guy on the planet. Not that I ever was, but I probably shut a lot of people out when they came around to welcome me back to town. I didn't want to sit around discussing my reasons for leaving the DEA."

"I get it." She understood the desire for privacy. It was easier to close off than to engage. She had done the same thing herself after Ali died. She'd probably pushed quite a few people away, but she needed to deal with the sadness on her own.

Gideon shook his head. "Still, I sure was glad to have help back there at the VFW. All those guys really came through for me, even the mayor. I'm just sorry I let that thug manhandle you that way." He gazed at her with such intensity that she needed to look away.

"You saved my life, Gideon. Those men would have killed me if you hadn't been there." A piece of wood crackled in the stove, and despite the warmth of the fire, she hugged her arms to her chest and bit her lip to keep her teeth from chattering.

"You're shivering." Gideon pulled a blanket off one of the bunks and draped it around her shoulders. It helped. A little.

She gave herself a pep talk. Yes, it was freezing, but Gideon had to be as cold as she was. Colder even. He had been in the front of the snowmobile, facing off with the worst of the wind and blowing snow, and he wasn't complaining. And, as he said, it wouldn't take long for the icehouse to warm up. She closed her eyes and tried picturing herself on a blanket on a sunny beach. The sand tickling her toes as a bead of sweat rolled down her face, and...

It wasn't working. Her legs shook convulsively. When she opened her eyes, Gideon was standing beside her, a pile of blankets in his hands.

"Your lips are blue," he said.

Not the kind of compliment a woman wanted to hear. But how could she complain when he tucked one of the blankets under her legs and layered the second across her shoulders?

Gideon waited until she was comfortable and then walked toward the cot on the south wall, crouched down and fished his arm underneath the frame. It didn't take long for him to find what he was looking for: a cardboard shoebox with a rubber band holding the lid in place. Inside the box was a gun.

As he gazed at the pistol, Gideon wore the look of a man recognizing an old friend. A half smile played on his lips as he checked the chamber and ejected the magazine. The moment seemed so intensely private that she pressed her eyelids together and tried to imagine what was going on at the reservation. Tonight was the big celebration at the community center, and the kids had been excited to take part in the ceremony. She wished she could be with them, taking pictures and offering support. Instead, she was sitting in an icehouse and trying not to think about the drugs or the sheriff or the two men from the SUV.

She opened her eyes just in time to see Gideon set the gun back into the box. He noticed her watching and leaned forward on his chair. "Now all I need are some answers from my buddy at the DOJ. That can wait until we're back onshore. You need to warm up before we venture outside again."

"I'm fine." She concentrated hard on keeping her voice steady and sure. "I'm ready to go when you are."

He shook his head. "No. You're so cold that your lips can barely form words. We'll give the stove another half hour to warm this place up and then see how you feel."

There was a long silence. Gideon pulled out his phone a third time and held it above his head, but it was clear from his frustrated sigh that he still wasn't getting any reception.

"Why don't I stay here while you go and call your friend?" She pulled the blanket closer to her chest. Gideon's attempts to control his restlessness were making her anxious. "If it would help convince you, you can leave me your gun."

He raised a brow.

"What? You think I don't know how to use it? I took a gun safety course at the local range. I even got a certificate."

"When was that?"

"A while ago. But I remember the basics."

He reached down and lifted the pistol out of the shoebox. He held it for a moment, checked to make sure the safety was on and passed it to her.

She tucked it under one of the blankets on her

lap as he moved across the room and lifted a bow and quiver of arrows from the wall.

He caught her surprised look and shrugged. "This time of year, there's a chance there'll be wolves on the lake."

Tears threatened to overwhelm her as she thought about being alone in the icehouse. And the prospect of a pack of hungry wolves lurking nearby only heightened her anxiety. She shivered and then took a deep breath. "Be safe, okay?"

"Sure thing," he said as he slung the bow over one shoulder and the quiver over the other and headed out the door.

It took fifteen minutes to reach the shore. Five more to find a spot where he could get reception on his phone. Only two bars, but that was enough. Gideon was already second-guessing his decision to leave Dani alone out on the lake, but the sooner he got answers the better.

As he approached the embankment, a sudden movement in the trees caught his eye, and he reached up to touch the bow on his shoulder. But except for a lone fox scampering across the ice, the area was ominously quiet, with no signs of life.

He pulled over by the side of the road and opened his phone. There were two voice mails, both from Mike, his contact at the DOJ, confirming that new DNA evidence was scheduled to be presented in the trial of an Iowa politician accused of vehicular homicide and fleeing the scene.

It wasn't much, but it was a start.

Mike said he'd do a little digging to see if he could discover the name of the lab that had done the test on the politician's DNA. *Sit tight*, Mike had advised. *I've put in a call to a buddy of mine who's a DA in Des Moines. He was reluctant to say much on the phone, but he'd be willing to meet you if you come to Iowa. There's definitely something big going on. I'll have some answers for you by Monday at the close of the day.*

But sitting tight was not really an option, not with the sheriff on their tail and the threat of the two brutes who had tried to assault Dani. Besides, it was Saturday night, which meant they were two full days away from making any headway in the case. Gideon had learned early in his career that going back to the beginning was often the best way to make sense of the end. Which meant that, as soon as Dani had warmed up and was ready to travel, they needed to go to Iowa to talk to Mike's friend.

He paused with his hand on the throttle and strained his ears to listen to the distant roar of something or someone barreling down the road.

Before he could react, a large vehicle bumped off the tarmac and skidded onto the ice.

A tan SUV.

The driver must not have seen Gideon where he was hidden in the shadows. But the headlights of the vehicle illuminated the snowmobile's tracks on the lake.

Tracks that would lead straight to the icehouse where Dani was waiting.

THIRTEEN

According to the thermometer on the wall, the temperature of the icehouse had warmed to thirty-eight degrees. But frost still lingered in the air, refusing to give ground to the crackling fire.

Dani shifted her chair closer to the potbellied stove and tried to flex her toes and fingers, but they continued to feel numb from the cold. Never again would she complain about Iowa winters. Her teeth chattered as she clutched her arms around her chest. She tried thinking again of warm things—a steaming cup of coffee, a ninety-eight-degree summer day. But nothing could eliminate the chill.

BAM!

A noise jarred her senses as the north wall of the icehouse splintered like a balsa-wood airplane in the hands of a child.

Before she could react, a second blast shook the walls. Boxes and cans tumbled from shelves.

Picture frames slipped from the wall. The lanterns flickered as they slid across the table and crashed to the floor, plunging the room into darkness.

The sickly sweet tang of kerosene assailed her nostrils as the oil from the lanterns soaked the boards under her feet. Nausea rocked her stomach at the horror of a fire breaking out in the confined space. Even worse would be the shock of an icy plunge through the icehouse floor into the frigid waters of the lake.

There was a brief moment of silence, and then a third collision battered the house. Shards of wood rained down from the ceiling, landing on her shoulders and on top of her head.

The floor jerked forward and then back again as the structure jittered across the ice. The chair slid out from under her, knocking her to the floor. She pushed herself up on her knees and tried to stand, but she couldn't gain footing against the accelerating force.

Someone was deliberately ramming the icehouse with her trapped inside. She shivered convulsively, more from fear than cold. If the walls collapsed, she'd be buried alive under a pile of rubble and wood. Desperate, she looped her arm around the edge of the table and pulled herself upright. But the floor shifted again and her legs crumpled, knocking her back to her knees.

A spark in the stove sizzled, and a flame jumped up like a tongue of fire. One wrong move, and the kerosene could ignite. Time was running out. She needed to do something fast.

Her gaze fell on the pistol that had tumbled from her lap when she fell out of the chair. She traced her hand along the floorboards until she touched the cool hard metal of the barrel, and then she tucked the weapon into the waistband of her pants.

BAM!

Her hand wobbled as another boom sent shockwaves across the floor. She paused a moment to gain her bearings. Then, slowly and carefully, she crawled toward the door.

Her fingers jammed against the debris, her woolen gloves offering little protection against the shards of glass and plaster that littered the floor. She grasped the knob and pulled herself up to stand. With a heave, she pushed the door open and stepped onto the threshold, using her arms for support.

Against a black canvas of dark sky, the moon was like a spotlight illuminating the lake as the structure plowed forward, churning up a spray of powdery flakes. She brushed a veil of snow from her eyes and looked in horror as the icehouse slid closer and closer toward a line of rocks along the shore. She estimated that she had less than sixty seconds before it smashed into the jagged outcroppings.

Her options dwindled in the seconds it took to catch her breath.

She had to jump. It was the only way. But if her leap was short, she would be crushed under the moving structure before she could escape.

She clutched the sides of the door frame and prayed for courage.

It was now or never.

One, two, three… Go.

She pushed off from the door, angling her body to the left. Seconds passed as she fell through the air, hit the ground and tumbled and rolled, turning over and over as the icehouse rumbled past her, missing her by inches as it sped toward the rocks.

Relief flooded her senses. She closed her eyes, too frightened to move.

She was alive, but for how long?

Slivers of ice flew across the windshield of the snowmobile, pelting Gideon's face and chest. His fingers were raw. His throat was dry. His heart was racing. It didn't matter. Nothing mattered but saving Dani.

Fifty yards in front of him, the driver of the SUV revved the motor and prepared for a final blow. The air was split with a crack as the bum-

per rammed the icehouse wall. A second crash
followed the first as the vehicle accelerated, butt-
ing the structure forward only inches from the
rocks. Gideon tried to imagine Dani, huddled inside with no clue what was going on. She had a
gun, but that wouldn't help her unless she found
a way to escape.

An unpleasant sense of déjà vu dimmed his
senses. For the second time in two years, he'd
failed to protect a person who'd placed her life
in his hands. For the second moment in a lifetime, he found himself on the outside, watching
helplessly as the drama unfolded around him.

A flash in the distance caught his eye. Something lying in a heap on the snow. Dani! He'd
recognize the purple coat anywhere. Happiness
surged through his being, but just as quickly
slipped away. Was she alive? She wasn't moving, but then—his gaze flashed across her prone
body as her leg twitched and she moved her head.

He wanted to rush to her side, to lift her into
his arms and carry her to safety. But first, he
needed to deal with the men in the tan SUV. He
was closer now, just ten yards from their vehicle.
Close enough to attempt a shot. Standing up, he
pushed his knees against the steering column of
the snowmobile as his right foot pushed the accelerator to full throttle. He tipped the bow so

that he could place the shaft of the arrow on the shelf. Nocked the arrow and drew back the bow.

His first shot went wide, but he pulled another arrow from the quiver and steadied his hand to try again. His fingers stiff from frostbite, he drew back the bow, and this time, he hit his target—the left back tire of the SUV.

The vehicle swerved sideways and then righted itself. But he was ready with a third arrow, which tore through the rubber of the right tire.

The driver pointed a gun out the window and fired a shot that grazed the side of the snowmobile. The second man stuck his head out the other side of the vehicle and yelled something into the wind. Metal glinted against the door frame as he took aim.

There was only one arrow left in his quiver, and he needed to make it count.

He drew back his bow and took aim at the third tire. But it wasn't the zigzagging SUV that claimed his attention. It was Dani, struggling to pull herself upright on the ice.

If he could see her, the men could, too. She was a stationary target for both of their guns.

Dread choked him. "Get down!" he yelled.

She either heard him or slipped because seconds later she was once again lying flat on the lake.

The driver shifted into Reverse and backed away from the icehouse. The wheel bearings of the SUV scraped the ice with a screech as the vehicle did a three-point turn and headed straight for Dani.

Gideon held his breath as he nocked his arrow, drew back his bow and released his final shot.

Bull's-eye. A black piece of rubber flew through the air as his arrow tore through the third tire.

The SUV did a wide three-sixty, careening in a circle of gray smoke as the rims of the wheels carved deep gashes in the ice before slamming into a chunk of metal that had fallen from the icehouse roof.

Gideon slung his bow back over his shoulder and slowed to a stop two feet from Dani.

"Dani," he said. He was breathing so hard he could barely speak.

"Here." She pulled the pistol from the waistband of her pants and tossed it to him.

He caught the weapon and sprinted toward the disabled SUV where the two men were pinned under a pair of deflated airbags.

"Hands in the air," he shouted, training his gun on the disoriented driver.

The man pushed aside a tangle of white cloth and did as requested. His passenger followed suit, glaring his disdain through dark beady eyes.

"Leave us alone, man. We have no beef with you. We just want to talk to the girl."

Gideon reached into the vehicle and collected the weapons that had been tossed to the floor. "You have an odd way of initiating a conversation."

Dani appeared beside him. Her face was pale and drawn, but there was fire in her eyes as she stared down her tormentors.

"Hey, we just wanted to get her attention." The beefier thug spit out his words as if they were poison.

"Well, you've got mine," Gideon said. "For starters, you can explain why you planted drugs in the van."

The driver smirked. "Four words, man. Talk to my lawyer. That's all I have to say."

"Fine." Gideon choked down his anger as he yanked both men out of the SUV and marched them toward the icehouse with Dani trailing behind.

Inside the broken-down shack, he found a pile of bungee cords, which he used to secure the prisoners to the still-intact bunk that was welded to the floor. It was primitive, but it would do for the moment, or at least until Cal arrived to retrieve the prisoners.

"See you in court," Gideon said, motioning that Dani should follow him toward the snowmobile.

The driver's laughter was quick and mocking. "This isn't over, man. Just wait and see."

FOURTEEN

From the sounds drifting through the doors of the VFW banquet hall, the party inside was still going strong as Dani trailed Gideon across the lot toward a row of cars parked closest to the street. The police cars were gone, and Abby's friend's car was only a click of the lock away. As she climbed into the passenger seat of an old Crown Vic, Gideon slid behind the wheel, cranked up the heater and backed out of the space.

The warm air blowing out of the vents felt familiar and comforting, and for the first time in two hours, she could feel herself beginning to unclench her body. The ride to shore had been even more unnerving than the ride out to the icehouse. Gideon had cranked the snowmobile to top speed, and she could sense his urgency in the taut muscles on his back. But exchanging a snowmobile for a car was a definite upgrade for the journey ahead.

"Dani?" Gideon was frowning as they approached the intersection leading out of town. "Are you sure you're not hurt?"

She nodded. "I'm fine. I landed my jump in a pile of snow."

His brow furrowed. "I should never have left you alone."

"You didn't know that our hiding place was vulnerable."

"Maybe. But I'm sorry to have put you through that."

His eyes locked on hers, and she thought for a moment that he was going to say something more about the icehouse. But headlights in the rearview mirror caused him to lean forward and white-knuckle the wheel.

"It might be best if you stay low, at least until we get onto the highway. Can you toss me that cap from the back seat?"

She had to stretch to reach the navy ball cap with a Minnesota Twins logo, which lay on the shelf above the seat. Gideon pulled it down on his head as she slid to the floor and pressed her head against the cool, soft leather of the passenger seat. "Where are we going? To talk to the sheriff?"

"No. We're headed to Iowa. My friend at the DOJ gave me the name of a classmate of his from law school who works as a DA. I'm hoping either he or one of his colleagues can share some information about the Ravelli case. But before anything else, I suppose I better call Cal."

He took a wide turn, and she braced herself against the door as he pulled over to the side of the road. He slipped his phone out of the back pocket of his pants and punched in a number.

"Sheriff, this is Gideon Marshall. I left two men who were trying to kill Dani Jones tied up in Reg's smashed-up icehouse on the lake. You'll be able to figure out which one." He listened for a moment. "Right… Right… I get that you'd like to continue the conversation with Miss Jones, but it doesn't look like it's going to happen anytime soon. I'm not sure how much you'll be able to get from those two thugs, once they're all lawyered up, but I can personally testify to the fact that they tried to push Reg's icehouse into the rocks with her inside… Yup… Sure… Yup… I hear you, and I'll be sure to give that some serious thought. See you later." He clicked off and tossed down the phone onto the console.

She looked up at him. "Did the sheriff tell you to bring me in for questioning?"

"Sure. I told him I'd think about it, which I'll do as soon as I talk to the DA."

"Is Reg going to get in trouble for letting us hide at his place?"

"Nah. You haven't been charged with anything at this point, so he's in the clear."

She supposed that was true, but it didn't seem far-fetched to imagine that anyone who had helped them would eventually have to answer to the sheriff. "Where in Iowa are we going?"

"Des Moines." He covered his mouth to hide a yawn.

She did the calculation in her head. The clock on the dash said nine fifteen. Seven hours to the Iowa border, then another couple more to Des Moines. It would be a long drive in the middle of the night.

"We'll arrive sometime around eight in the morning?"

"Sounds right. Given the circumstances, I'd rather not spend any more time around here."

That made two of them. Even so, the thought of leaving Dagger Lake caused a heavy sadness to tug at her heart. A lump stuck in her throat as she imagined what the kids would think when they heard about her hurried escape. Would it make any sense to them? How could it, when she herself didn't understand?

"How do you think the men found us at the icehouse?"

Gideon shrugged. "I'm not sure. Maybe they heard someone mention that Reg had given me the keys to his snowmobile and followed our tracks on the lake. I'm just glad we won't have to worry about those two thugs any longer." He yawned again.

He looked exhausted. He had to be operating on sheer adrenaline and willpower.

She tapped him on the arm. "What would you say to letting me take the first shift? I saw a sign for a rest stop coming up in a few miles. We can change drivers there."

"Nah. I'm fine. You catch some shut-eye."

"But I took that nap back at Abby's neighbor's house. I don't think I'll be able to sleep." Being at Kenny's felt like a lifetime ago. "Besides, I like driving at night. You can take a turn when we stop for gas."

They switched seats at the next rest stop. At first, Gideon seemed determined to stay awake for the duration of her turn at the wheel. But then, like a balloon that had been slowly losing air, he suddenly deflated. His head bumped against the window, and when she looked over to check on him, his eyes had blinked shut. But even as he dozed, he hadn't completely given up the fight. His lips were curled in a disaffected frown, and his eyelids twitched every time she reset the cruise control. It was as if he might spring into wakefulness at any minute and offer a critique of her driving. A sign on the right side of highway announced that they were entering

Fargo. In a couple of minutes, they'd be crossing the Red River into Minnesota, which would mean that they'd be one state away from Cal Stanek and the long arm of the Dagger Lake law.

Gideon remained fast asleep. He had pushed his seat back as far as it could go, but he still managed to resemble a grumpy old grizzly stuck in a cage.

As she drove across the bridge, she tapped the brakes to take her speed down a notch. She could really go for a hot cup of coffee and maybe some music to help pass the time. She thought about the drive out to North Dakota and the cheerful companionship of her small group of teens. She had found a radio station that was playing Christmas music, and they'd all had fun singing along. Maybe she could find the call number of that station again.

As she reached for the dial, Gideon opened one eye. "I think it's time I took over. Don't we need gas or something?"

"We're okay for a while," she reported with a frown. Apparently, Gideon was one of those people who filled up every time the gauge dipped close to the halfway mark.

"Let's stop at the next gas station to fill the tank." His voice was still thick with sleep. "Where are we, anyway?"

"A little past Moorhead. But keep sleeping. I'm doing fine."

He closed his eyes again, and two minutes later, began to snore.

It appeared that there would be no coffee or music for the duration of her time at the wheel. Just the wide-open road and a kaleidoscope of thoughts clamoring in her head.

Gideon woke up when Dani stopped to get gas. The air inside the car was stale with recycled heat, and his neck was stiff and tight with tension. Even so, he felt less groggy than expected after a four-hour nap.

But Dani looked beat. He could see her through the windshield, leaning against the side of the car as she pumped the gas. Sliding into the driver's seat, he let Dani climb into the back to nap. He watched through the mirror as she folded her body across the seat, curled and uncurled her knees as she searched for a comfortable position.

After an hour, he could see that she had finally fallen asleep. He twisted the angle of the rearview mirror so he could check on her while she slept. Her eyes were closed, and her breathing was slow and regular.

She was perfect, inside and out. Brave, tenacious and strong. When he was with her, his heart beat a little faster. And an urge to protect her welled up in his chest. He hadn't felt this way about a woman for a long time, and he wasn't sure that he liked where it was headed.

It just wasn't worth it to love someone too much.

He had vowed to never leave his heart vulnerable to those kinds of feelings, even if it meant living the rest of his life alone. The events that had unfolded at the DEA two years ago weren't the only reason he had closed himself off from the rest of the world. It was a decision he had made years ago, and the tragedy with his murdered witness had only cemented his resolve.

He could still close his eyes and remember the feeling of bewilderment when his mother explained to him that his father had been killed in a car accident. At that moment, it had felt like his world ended.

In a lot of ways, it had.

His mom hadn't been able to cope with her grief and the challenges of raising two small children on her own. So she'd packed up the family and moved back to Dagger Lake, to the house on the reservation where she'd grown up.

Gone was the proud feeling of being lifted up high on his father's broad shoulders in the backyard of their snug little cottage in their charming college town. Gone were the tree-lined boulevards and friendly students who would lounge on the porch swing and chat. And gone forever was the laughter in his young mother's eyes.

In place of a home full of happy memories was a house with distant relatives, bleak landscapes and tears.

Lots of tears.

It had been hard finding his place in the community. His father had been white, and his mother was Sioux. In the classroom, at church and on the playground, he didn't fit in either world.

He wondered if he ever would.

Abby would bust his chops if she heard him say that. Especially given all the help he had just received from her friends on the reservation. But that was the thing. They were *her* friends, not his. He was a loner. He didn't need anyone.

Not even Dani.

But even against the strength of his resolve, the thought of someone hurting her made him see red. He would keep her safe and help her clear her name. But that was all.

He rolled down his window and let a blast of frigid air cool his emotions. Outside, the sky was black, but in the distance, he could see the lights of the city. He pulled off the highway just outside Minneapolis a little after 3:00 a.m. He needed to get gas and something to eat. The familiar hunger that he recalled from so many all-nighters on the job gnawed at his stomach, and he considered the efficiency of a burrito breakfast to go.

As the tires of the Crown Vic crunched against the gravel of the all-night truck stop, he realized this was the first time in weeks that he was parking on pavement that was free of snow.

It was a cheering thought. At least for the moment, they had reached civilization, Northern-style.

"Gideon?"

Dani's face appeared between the seats, her hair tousled and her eyes drowsy. He fought the temptation to reach over and kiss the top of her head.

"Hi there." Did his voice sound as smitten to her ears as it did to his? He needed to work harder in keeping his feelings in check. "Hungry?"

She offered a sleepy nod. "Starved. I wouldn't say no to a cup of coffee and breakfast with all the fixings."

So much for the burrito breakfast to go.

Five minutes later, they grabbed a corner booth and placed identical orders for the special. When the waitress returned with their food, Dani folded her napkin across her lap, bowed her head and prayed. "Father God. Thank You for protecting us through our journey. Bless this food and the other drivers all around us and please keep everyone safe on the road ahead. In Jesus's name we pray. Amen."

Gideon shook his head.

"Is everything okay?" she asked.

"Fine," he said. "I'm just amazed that after everything that's happened to you, you still make time to pray."

She seemed stunned by his statement. "Of course. That's the important stuff. Thanking God for His gifts, not always complaining about the crosses that come our way."

"Sorry. I don't get it. You just had a near-death experience. It's hard for me to understand what you have to be thankful for."

He knew he sounded confrontational, but Dani's blind faith in God's protection seemed naive. He had seen too much to trust in a loving Savior.

She reached across the table and took his hand. "It's complicated and simple at the same time. Maybe I could tell you a story that illustrates my point. A few days after Ali was murdered, my mom made dinner, but naturally, no one wanted to eat. I actually remember thinking that I would never enjoy another meal again. My dad took my hand and my mom's and began to thank God for the food that was before us on the table. He talked about how much we were going to miss Ali, especially when we were gathered together for meals, but how happy we would all be when we were able to join hands with her in heaven. It was hard to sit there and act like everything was normal when it was as opposite of that as you could get. See? Complicated because it hurt to think about how much we all missed Ali, but easy, because it meant we trusted in our Savior. My dad knew even during our darkest hour that our faith was the only thing that could get us through the sadness." She released his hand and smiled.

"Did it?" he asked.

"Definitely."

He wished he could share in that certainty. Dani leaned her head against the side of the booth, a faraway look in her eyes. Was she thinking about her sister? Her faith had helped heal the wound, but the pain was still etched in her features.

"Tell me about Ali," he said.

Dani shook her head, and, for a minute, he thought she wasn't going to respond. But then she did.

"Ali was a fighter. If she were here, she'd want to figure out why I was being targeted. She was super smart, very analytical and logical. When we were in school, I had to work really hard just to keep up with her."

"You're smart."

"Not like Ali. She'd finish her homework and then help me with mine. She was always going the whole nine yards for the people she loved."

"She sounds like you."

Dani shrugged. "That's kind of you to say, but I'm not sure it's true. Sometimes, when I'm stuck on something, I ask myself what Ali would do. About a year after she died, I let myself get talked into going to a school dance. I wasn't ready to go out, but I knew it was something Ali would have wanted. And my parents encouraged me to let go of my grief and have fun."

"Did you?"

She nodded. "For a while. But I didn't like the way it made me feel. Like I was moving on and leaving an important part of myself behind. That night after the dance, I went home and began to make a plan for what I wanted to do with the rest of my life. I decided I needed to work harder in school, study more and be more purposeful about the choices I made."

Wow. That was a heavy burden for a fourteen-year-old. Dani had been through so much, but Gideon had never heard her complain. Instead, she had focused her energies on the positive. It didn't take a rocket scientist to recognize that the teens she worked with in her church's ministry were close to the age her sister had been when she was abducted. And Ali's death had been the catalyst that inspired her to become a DNA researcher.

In some ways, he and Dani were alike. At an early age, Dani had lost her sister, and he had lost his dad. But the similarity ended there. Dani had taken the tragedy and turned it for good. He had done the opposite. As a fatherless child growing up on the reservation, he had turned his back on God and embraced the role of an outcast. And the events that had happened in Miami two years ago had only further hardened his heart.

He paid the check and they walked back to the car. Dani seemed deflated by their conversation, and he resolved not to press her any more about the circumstances of Ali's death.

But a short time later, he considered asking Dani to start up again with the prayers when a set of whirling red lights shone in his rearview mirror.

Gideon pulled over and adjusted the angle of his mirror for a better view of the tall, gangly-legged man in the tan jacket and flat brim hat stepping out of the unmarked cruiser parked behind them on the side of the road. An all-too-real worst-case scenario played in his head as the patrolman approached the driver's side of the Crown Vic, scowling like a bloodhound who had spent half a day tracking the culprit who had stolen his dinner.

Rule number one when getting pulled over: always be polite, even when you're one hundred percent certain that you've been obeying the speed limit and following the rules of the road.

With the push of a button, Gideon lowered the window and leaned an elbow out into the cold.

"What can I do for you, Officer?" he asked with a forced smile.

"License and registration," the policeman barked. A thin, straight line formed between his eyebrows as he flashed a badge that identified him as Officer Tony McDonald. For all his bluster, he couldn't have been a day older than twenty-four.

With one hand, Gideon handed his license through the window and with the other, he reached down. He was counting on finding the registration information in the storage compartment under the seat. He held his breath as his hand flipped through a couple of maps and a pile of napkins, then exhaled a sigh of relief as his fingers grazed a plastic folder in the drawer. Maintaining eye contact, he handed the officer the paperwork containing the insurance card and vehicle registration for the Crown Vic. Beside him, Dani, looking small and terrified, slunk low in her seat and stared straight ahead. He wanted nothing more than to pull her close and offer her reassurances. They had made it this far. He wasn't going to fail her now.

The patrolman gave the information a cursory glance and then, without speaking a word, retraced his steps back to his vehicle.

"Why did he stop us?" Dani asked in a whisper, her eyes wide and worried. "Do you think he knows what happened at Dagger Lake?"

"I'm not sure." Gideon's voice was calm, the opposite of how he was feeling. "Right now, he's checking my license for priors. Let's just hope that Cal didn't put out a BOLO. If he did, we're definitely not going to make it to Des Moines today."

Dani fidgeted as they waited for the patrolman to return. Gideon's leg twitched, and for a moment he thought about putting the pedal to the metal and taking off down the highway. They were probably less than five minutes from the border. And the Crown Vic was fast. He was sure it could outdistance Officer McDonald's hunk-of-junk Chevy Caprice. At the very least, they would make it to the next exit before the cop car gave serious chase.

But before he could give in to the temptation to flee, Officer McDonald ambled back down the shoulder of the road, his face fixed in a somber frown.

"You've got a broken taillight on the rear right corner," the patrolman said, handing him his license. "Get it fixed first thing tomorrow, and there won't be a problem, okay?"

"I'll do that. Thanks." He looked over at Dani. She was sitting completely still and appeared to be waiting for the other shoe to drop.

But that was it.

There was no other shoe. Just the broken taillight. Sometimes things were as straightforward as they seemed. But just to make sure, he waited for the patrol car to pull out before merging back onto the road.

As the lights of the police vehicle faded into the traffic, Gideon heaved a sigh of relief. "Let's hope we can make it the last two hours to Des Moines without getting pulled over again."

"About that." Dani pointed to the clock on the dash "It's after five, and we're both exhausted. What do you think about making a stop at Blooming Prairie? We're less than fifteen minutes from my apartment, so we can pop in and wash up. Maybe take a quick shower and a short nap. And you could call your buddy's friend and set up a time to talk."

It wasn't a terrible idea. Gideon had been wondering what they'd do when they arrived in Des Moines at eight o'clock in the morning. Dani's proposal definitely had its appeal, though returning to her apartment did have risks. The thugs who were after her clearly knew where she lived. On the other hand, it was unlikely Ravelli's people knew of their whereabouts. As far as they were concerned, he and Dani were still in Dagger Lake.

"Okay," he agreed. "Give me directions to your place."

"Actually, what would you think about heading straight to the lab? It's only a few minutes from my apartment, and I could dash inside to see what I can find. The information about the cases is kept on my supervisor's computer. All I'd need to do is figure out her password to verify that I was the technician who did the test."

"No." He shook his head. "My contact in Des Moines will have access to the same information, and it won't involve breaking into the lab and hacking into a computer."

"But we wouldn't be breaking in. I work there, remember? I'm allowed to be inside the building anytime I want. We'll just need to stop at my apartment to pick up my badge. I can't get in or out of the building without it. Unless..." She paused. "A colleague of mine works a lot of overtime—weekends, early mornings and late nights. Why don't I give him a call and see if he's around? If he is, I can ask him to meet me at the door and get me through security. He might even be able to help find out if I'm scheduled to testify against Patrick Ravelli."

"I told you what I think. It's a bad idea."

"Let's just see if he's at the lab, and then we can plan from there." She picked up her phone and scrolled through her contacts. The battery light had turned red, but apparently there was enough juice left to make her call. From the tone of her voice, Gideon could tell she'd reached her friend's voice mail.

"Hi, Adam. It's Dani. Sorry to bother you so early on a Sunday morning. I'm on my way into town and I was thinking of stopping at the lab. But I don't have my badge. So, I thought if you happened to be on-site, you could come downstairs and get me through security. If you're not at work, no problem. I need to go back to my place anyway to take a shower and change. It's been a long couple of days with lots of excitement, which explains why I sound kind of hyper. I'll tell you the whole story when I see you on Monday. Thanks. Bye."

She clicked off and turned toward Gideon with an apologetic smile.

He let out a long breath through his nose. "Dani, I don't think you understand the gravity of the situation. I hope you're not expecting to make it back to work this week. The case won't be wrapped up that quickly, even if you find exactly what you're looking for at the lab."

"But once Cal talks to the two men who tried to wreck the icehouse, he can start an investigation to trace the cocaine to Patrick Ravelli. Then I won't be his number one suspect anymore."

Gideon shook his head.

In his experience, these things were never that simple. One problem would follow another as investigators sifted through the evidence linking the hit-and-run to the cocaine. There would be motions to compel, motions to strike, all adding up to weeks and weeks of delay.

"I don't know, Dani." His voice was weary as he considered the obstacles still ahead of them. "I wouldn't count on going back to Danford until we've identified all the people behind this scheme to take you down."

The words of the thug at the icehouse flashed across his brain. It wasn't over. That was clear. And the closer they got to Dani's hometown, the more present the danger and the more terrifying the risks.

FIFTEEN

Following Dani's instructions, Gideon took the next sharp right, which brought them to the front of her apartment building, a boxy old brownstone at the end of the block on Drexel Lane. After a five-hundred-mile journey across three states, she was finally home.

Whether it was exhaustion, stress or sentimentality, she didn't know, but the sight of the familiar block letters marking her address caused tears to form in her eyes. Blinking rapidly, she used the largest key on her ring to unlock the door.

Her apartment smelled like peaches, but not the fresh delicious kind that filled the bins of the farmers market in the middle of summer. It was more like the artificial scent of fruit-flavored gum, emanating from a pink three-wicked candle that had spent the last four days stewing by the heating vent in the dining room.

She waited for Gideon to say something about

the odor, but his face remained impassive as he followed her inside the apartment.

Dani might have been projecting her own feelings about the mess, but it seemed that his gaze swept across the living room, taking in the mismatched wicker chairs and her tattered magenta couch with the missing cushion that she planned to restuff as soon as she found the time, lingering for a moment on the old brown Schwinn that she'd left leaning against the entry wall. The last time she used it was back in September, but she had neglected to return it to the storage room where tenants kept their bikes.

Magazines littered the floor, dishes were stacked in the sink and an open bag of tortilla chips spilled onto the coffee table, remnants of the hurried snack she had consumed the night before leaving for Dagger Lake.

It was embarrassing.

Especially since Gideon's place was so smart and neat.

It was hardly a good excuse, but she had been extra busy in the days leading up to the mission trip to the reservation. Twelve-hour shifts at the lab hadn't left much time for cleaning the apartment.

"Can I get you anything to eat?" she asked, sliding a scoopful of chips into the trash can and then shoving the bag into a cabinet. "I can make you some…um…toast if you're hungry."

"I'm good," he said.

With a slow, deliberate gait, he walked toward her, and for a moment, in her exhausted state of mind, with her senses in frenzied overdrive, she thought he was going to kiss her.

Instead, he reached across the counter and picked up her Danford ID tag, which was lying on top of a jumble of papers and mail. "Cute picture," he said. "Why don't you go ahead and take that shower you've been talking about while I fire up your computer and see if I can find any other pertinent facts about Senator Ravelli."

"Okay." She reached across the counter and plugged her cell into the charger. Then she grabbed a fresh towel from the linen closet and headed to the bathroom.

Now that Gideon had seen the inside of her apartment, he seemed different. Warier. More reserved. It was possible that he was disappointed that her place wasn't posh or that her decorating bordered on shabby chic. But to be fair, he had been acting strangely even before they walked in the door.

Or maybe it was her. Now that they were on her home turf she felt a greater need to assert her independence. Everything she had worked for, all of her long-term plans and careful lists, hung in the balance. Gideon had gotten them this far, but he was exhausted. This was her town. DNA was her field of expertise. She couldn't sit back and let him do everything.

There were still loose ends to tie up before they could prove her innocence. Talking about going back to her job was just a way of distracting herself from the obstacles that lay ahead.

Gideon didn't need to tell her the lead to Patrick Ravelli was a long shot and might prove to be a dead end. If that happened, then what? Would she be a fugitive forever, moving from city to city with a false identity as she struggled to clear her name? It wasn't just her reputation at stake. She could lose almost everything she loved and held dear.

Gideon pulled up a chair and turned on Dani's computer, tapping into a website detailing Patrick Ravelli's history. He had read it before, but it seemed like a good idea to scroll through the details a second time, hoping something would leap out at him. Though it was hardly the most reliable source, it did do a decent job of chronicling Ravelli's life and meteoric rise to his current position in the state senate.

Patrick James Ravelli was born in Waterloo, Iowa. His father was a prominent businessman; his mother, a homemaker. He'd graduated from Harvard at eighteen and received his JD at twenty-one, so he was obviously a pretty smart guy. It must have been a surprise to everyone when he returned home and accepted a job as an assistant city attorney, a position he used as a springboard in the election to his current post.

Gideon skimmed over the stuff about Ravelli's wife and family, reading between the lines for signs that the man was a political hack, but despite all his advantages, Ravelli seemed like a decent sort of guy. Active in his church and community, volunteer at a soup kitchen. Not to mention chairman of the board of a foundation that helped immigrants find jobs and housing in the Des Moines area.

That was one of the reasons Ravelli's arrest for the hit-and-run accident that claimed the life of Veng Chrin had garnered so many headlines. Chrin, a Cambodian immigrant, had actually applied for assistance from Ravelli's foundation, an irony that hadn't been overlooked in local coverage of the accident.

Clicking out of the website, Gideon opened the Sunday edition of the *Des Moines Register*. The online report was similar to the stories he had read earlier. There was the same intriguing tease about an explosive DNA testimony scheduled to be revealed in the week ahead.

But there was no mention of Danford.

He read the story twice just to make sure. Then, he checked another news source, hoping for confirmation. This time, the information was even less helpful. The reporter speculated that the testing had been done at a lab in Memphis, Tennessee.

He pushed back in the chair and blew out a long sigh.

If the articles were accurate, it pretty much shot to pieces his theory about Dani being targeted because of her involvement in the Ravelli case.

Frustration washed over him. Things like this had happened regularly when he worked for the DEA. A lead wouldn't pan out, and he'd have to start over, reexamine the facts and reassess the evidence. It was all part of the job.

But this time it was different.

His dog had been stabbed.

His barn had burned down.

And he was bone weary with exhaustion and five hundred miles from home. Dani was counting on him, and he had let her down. He rubbed his eyes and stared at the article on the screen, hoping to find answers somewhere in the small print.

Maybe a shot of caffeine would clear his mind and help him focus. There was a coffee maker on the kitchen counter with a nest of filters stacked in a basket by its side. If he could find some beans, he could brew a pot of joe and begin the slow process of reviewing the facts for the umpteenth time.

"Dani?" he called through the bathroom door. The shower had been turned off, and he assumed she could hear him. "Is it okay if I make some coffee?"

"Wait and I'll do it." Her muffled response sounded like he had interrupted her in the middle of brushing her teeth. He squirted some dish-washing liquid into the sink and filled the basin with warm sudsy water. It wouldn't hurt to wash a few dishes while he waited, anything that would help him look at the situation through fresh eyes.

He dried the last mug and set it on the counter, then paced around the kitchen, trying to control his frustration. The answers had to be out there, if only he could see past all the distractions.

He opened the cabinet over the sink and found a large can of Folgers. As he measured out a portion of grounds, the scoop scraped against something soft and pliant. Gideon dug his hand deep, his fingers pressing against a plastic bag buried deep in the grounds. He knew what it was even before he saw it. In texture and consistency, it was identical to the stuff he had found in the van.

The bathroom door opened and Dani padded

toward him, her bare feet leaving a wet trail on the tile floor.

"I can make you that coffee now." Her smile faded as her gaze took in the open canister of coffee and the bag of white powder. "Is that...?"

He nodded. "More cocaine."

"Someone broke into my apartment?" There were damp patches on her shoulders where the ends of her wet hair had brushed against the fabric of her T-shirt, which, for some reason, made her appear all the more vulnerable.

"Yes," he said. His eyes darted around the apartment looking for clues. If he were still with the DEA, he could call in the crime scene investigators to dust the room for prints. As it was, he could only guess that the intruder had jimmied the less-than-high-tech lock on the apartment door.

A single teardrop ran down Dani's face. "Who's doing this to me?"

He shook his head. "I'm not sure." If only he had a clearer picture of what was going on. It was possible that the two men from the tan SUV had planted the drugs before they left for Dagger Lake. But why?

Dani clenched her fingers into tight fists. "We should go to the lab right now. Get this thing settled, once and for all. I'm tired of not knowing what's going on."

He put a restraining hand on her arm. "I think we should wait."

"Why?" she demanded. "Why let this drag on any longer than it has to? We know what we're looking for. Why delay?" Her eyes begged him to explain.

"Nothing about this case makes any sense, Dani. Every time it feels like we're moving forward, something happens to knock us back. At this point, I think we need to consider other options."

She tilted her head sideways. "What do you mean, other options? Has something happened to put the brakes on pursuing the lead to Patrick Ravelli?"

He was relieved she'd been the one to bring it up. "I was hoping to wait to tell you this, but the local papers are claiming the DNA testing was by a lab in Tennessee. Danford wasn't mentioned."

"That's typical." Dani's voice was tinged with hysteria. "The newspapers always speculate after getting stonewalled by the police. The fact that no one has mentioned Danford doesn't mean anything."

He shrugged. "If you say so."

"I do say so because I know from experience that it's true. This kind of thing happens all the time, especially in high-profile cases. My boss always says that in the world of DNA testing, too much publicity is a bad thing." She looked at him through defeated eyes. "I'm getting the feeling you don't believe me about this."

"I want to believe you. But…" He was too tired to fight, and he didn't want to argue with Dani, especially now as color rose up her cheeks in anger and she clenched her jaw with determination.

"But you don't. You've decided that some random reporter knows more about the situation than I do."

"Don't be ridiculous. That's not what I said."

"You're the one who is being ridiculous. You seem to be forgetting that trust is a two-way street. I trusted you throughout this entire ordeal. But now, all of a sudden, you're blaming me because someone planted drugs in my apartment."

"I'm not blaming you, Dani. More than anyone else, I understand how it feels to be set up for something you didn't do. But we need to be patient and let the experts handle this part of the investigation." He knew his voice sounded strained, but he was too tired to make the necessary effort to convince her of something he wasn't even sure he believed himself. Plus, she was twisting his words and overreacting to everything he said. He wasn't trying to accuse her or imply she knew about the cocaine. More than anything, he just wanted to keep her safe. He raised his hands in surrender. "We're both exhausted and frustrated, and we're saying things that neither of us means."

"Fine." She reached into a basket and tossed him a pillow and a light throw. "You take the couch, and I'll take the bed. We can talk about it in a couple of hours after we get some sleep."

SIXTEEN

Dani put her ear to the door and listened. With all the adrenaline surging through her system, she hadn't been able to settle down, but the sound of muffled snoring confirmed that, at least for the moment, Gideon was asleep. Tiptoeing into the living room, she snagged her security badge and the keys to the Crown Vic from the coffee table by the couch, then headed out the door.

If all went well, she'd be back before he realized she was gone.

No doubt about it, he'd be mad to discover that she had sneaked out of the apartment without giving him a heads-up on her plan. But the way she looked at it, she didn't have much choice. Maybe what the paper said about the testing being done in Memphis was true, and maybe it wasn't. There was only one way to find out. She needed to access her boss's computer and check the schedule for the week ahead.

It wasn't that she didn't trust Gideon when he

said his contact had access to the same information, but she wasn't certain he understood the level of security at Danford. All their data was stored in on-site servers. They didn't use cloud technology or even off-site IT assistance. The confidentiality of their clients was too important.

She just prayed she could find the information she was looking for. And if it turned out she wasn't slated to testify in the Ravelli case, then they would need to find a different explanation for the smuggled cocaine.

No matter what happened, she had to clear her name. Whoever had planted the drugs in her apartment hadn't realized it would be the push she needed to spur her into action. She was tired of being victimized, tired of having her reputation torn to shreds.

For the first thirteen years of her life, she had been the easygoing twin, the passive sidekick to Ali's larger personality. Even after Ali's death, she had clung to that identity, hoping she'd retain some part of her sister. But it was time to stop living in the past. Ali would always be a part of her, but maybe instead of maintaining their childhood roles, she needed to adopt some of Ali's gumption. She needed to become an active participant in her own life.

Finding that last stash of drugs had been the catalyst for resetting the plan, at least as far as

Gideon was concerned. But it had just renewed Dani's conviction that the answer was at Danford. Still, she wished she could take back the words she'd said in the heat of the moment. But she'd been overwrought at the thought of an intruder breaking into her apartment, and she had spoken without thinking.

Traffic was light since it was Sunday morning, and she made the short drive to Danford in record time. She circled past the stone entrance of the Port Reyes Office Park toward a semicircle of identical tan-bricked structures and turned to the left. In front of the building leased by Danford, two pencil-shaped light fixtures on the exterior wall illuminated the address.

Fifteen Ten North Loop West.

She parked in one of the spaces in back. Wasn't that Adam's car she had seen when she drove past the front of the building? Maybe if he was around, he could help her break into Missy's computer.

She reached into her purse for her phone, but she came up empty, and in a flash of clarity, she remembered leaving it plugged into the charger on the counter at the apartment.

No matter. She didn't need it, anyway.

She followed the path to the entrance under a low-hanging awning still covered with snow.

Holding her badge in front of the scanner, she heard the telltale sound of the latch clicking open.

So far so good. She made her way into the reception area, a large open room with a glass desk at the front. A dim overhead light flickered as she hurried past the customer service center toward the elevator in the back of the building. Another quick swipe, and the gray doors whooshed open, and she stepped inside. The elevator jingled, the doors closed and, with a final quiver, it began its ascent.

There were butterflies in her stomach as she anticipated her next move. The security guard— an older man named James, who worked most weekend nights—made rounds once an hour, so she needed to plan carefully. James wouldn't be surprised to see her working early on a Sunday morning. But if he found her in one of the interior offices, poking around on someone else's computer, her presence would be harder to explain.

The elevator lurched past the second-floor storage center before coming to a stop on the third floor. The doors slid open to reveal a row of metal counters, gray and shiny in the dim fluorescent glow. She passed her own workstation, where a pile of paperwork awaited her return. Stacks of manila folders littered her desk next to a cube of yellow Post-it notes. She ignored the desire to tidy up and headed toward the offices along the far wall.

A shiver of apprehension ran up her spine as she reached the one belonging to Missy, her boss. The door was locked—she had expected that—but she also knew there was a spare key in the top drawer of Missy's secretary's desk.

She took a deep breath and tried to calm her jangled nerves. Her hand shook as she stepped behind the desk and slid open the drawer. As she was about to reach for the key, she heard the sound of footsteps padding down the hall. Muscles tight with apprehension, she froze in place. She waited a few moments, but she didn't hear anything more.

Dani palmed the key and quietly pushed the drawer back in place. Stepping around the desk, she pushed the key into the lock with trembling fingers. She turned it and the door swung open.

Now for the hard part.

She needed to access the schedule.

A week ago, she had been standing behind Missy when her boss had logged on to her computer. Usually, Missy's slow hunt-and-pecking typing frustrated her, but in this moment, she was thankful for the sneak peek at the boss's password. Dani raked her memory as she pictured Missy's fingers poised on the keys. "Parasol Four One…" *What came next?* She closed her eyes and concentrated. "Nine Pound." Two seconds later, the log-on screen cleared and the desktop blinked on. She was in.

Hastily, she clicked on the folder titled Testimony and opened the Word document labeled "Schedule for the third week in December."

Tuesday: Set to testify regarding Specimen 145FD3. Tester: Danika Jones.

Dani felt her heart leap in her chest as the first piece of the puzzle fell into place. She closed the document, then opened the ID log.

She scrolled through until she found the identity associated with Specimen 145FD3—Ravelli, Patrick J.

Dani staggered backward and bumped into a plant on the sideboard next to the desk. As she hastened to steady it, her arm brushed against the picture of Missy's kids, which toppled and shattered on the floor. As she bent to pick it up, one of the sharp bits of glass cut into her wrist, and a dribble of blood ran down her hand.

In a panic, she grabbed for the tissues on the desk, leaving a bloody smudge on the box. She was leaving fingerprints everywhere. Missy would know that someone had broken in to her office, and it wouldn't take long for investigators, examining the footage from cameras throughout the lab, to establish who that someone might be. But by that time, Dani ought to have answers that would explain her actions. At least, that was what she hoped.

Gideon woke up to the first chords of a familiar melody.

He listened for a minute, half-asleep. That quickly, the music stopped, but seconds later, it started again. This time he was awake enough to realize that the sound he was hearing was the ringtone on Dani's phone. He pulled himself up and looked around the room, his sensors on alert as he realized something was dreadfully wrong.

His trained eyes scanned the room, noticing the open bedroom door, the rumpled sheets and the empty bed.

The keys to the Crown Vic were missing.

So was Dani's Danford ID badge.

Dani had gone to the lab to investigate on her own.

He slammed his fist down in frustration.

If Dani took the car, he didn't even have a vehicle to follow her. He eyed the bike propped against the wall and considered whether or not it could hold the weight of a 230-pound man. Hadn't Dani claimed the lab was a straight shot from her apartment, a ten-minute drive on a good day? On the bike, he could probably cover the distance in twenty minutes or less.

Or he could call a cab. But who knew how long it would take to arrive, and at that point, Dani might have already returned to the apartment. He checked his Uber app and saw there were no cars nearby this early in the morning. Maybe the best course of action would be to stay and wait.

A red light blinked on Dani's cell phone. One missed call, at 5:55 a.m., from someone named Adam Zajac. He pressed Play and listened.

"Hey, Dani. It's AZ. Your favorite coworker. I just got your message, and I'm extremely intrigued, trying to figure out why you would come back from vacation and head to work." There was a malicious laugh and then he continued. "In any case, I'm actually here at Danford right now, downstairs in the storage center. I heard some noises coming from the third floor, and I was about to go investigate. But then it occurred to me that it might be you. Give me a call and let me know what's up. See ya…"

The sickly sweet sarcastic tone on the other end of the line made Gideon's blood run cold. Did AZ know more than he was letting on? It was a chance he couldn't take.

He dropped the phone and hoisted the bike off the wall.

* * *

Dani reached across Missy's credenza and clicked Print. Her wrist was still bleeding, so she wrapped another tissue around the cut to prevent it from soaking through.

She stared at the paper tray and waited. Once she had a copy of the schedule, she'd have solid proof that Gideon was right about Patrick Ravelli. But, as usual, the printer was on the fritz, blinking a warning message with an imperious red light. Out of Paper, its usual excuse for not performing the assigned task. Grabbing a sheaf of copy paper from the ream on the shelf below, she flipped open the drawer and shoved a handful of sheets inside.

She waited for the feed to reset.

As she stood by the desk, willing the printer to engage, she again heard the sound of muffled footsteps approaching from the other end of the hall. Pulse racing, she shoved the printer drawer shut, turned off the lights and slunk down to the floor. It was probably just James making his usual rounds, nothing more ominous than that.

The sound of footsteps grew louder.

She held her breath as the person stopped in front of Missy's door. But as the footsteps continued down the hallway, she slowly released it. She was safe.

The printer beeped twice and began to engage.

The footsteps paused, and she froze in place.

Eyes closed tight, blood pounding in her veins, she waited helplessly as the door creaked open. The intruder flicked the switch, flooding the room in white light. Prickles of fear crept up her arm. She opened her eyes just in time to see a pair of neon sneakers heading toward the printer.

James did not wear sneakers.

A scream rose in her throat as the feet paused and then circled toward the desk. The intruder stopped in front of her. Slowly, he bent down, and a familiar face appeared.

SEVENTEEN

Relief washed over her as Dani scrambled up off the floor. The man standing in front of her, in basketball shorts and an Iowa State T-shirt, was Adam Zajac, her closest friend at Danford.

"Adam! I'm so glad it's you!" She brushed dust from the carpet off the knees of her jeans. "I heard footsteps, and I thought it was James. I was rehearsing what I was going to say to explain my reasons for snooping around in Missy's office."

He raised an inquiring brow. "Which are…?"

She opened her mouth to speak, but she couldn't find the words as she looked into the curious eyes of her friend. Her legs buckled under her as she slid down onto the seat of her boss's ergonomic chair.

"Oh, Adam. It's been a crazy couple of days. I left a message on your phone because I thought you might be in the office." She looked up and gave him a warm smile. "Turns out I was right."

"You know me, pal. Nose to the grindstone. Stuck on the treadmill. Burning the candle at both ends."

Dani laughed. Adam always joked that the two of them logged more overtime than the rest of their coworkers combined.

Adam pushed aside a pile of papers and perched next to her on the desk. "So, what are you doing here? And why are you back so early from your vacation?"

"I told you before I left. It wasn't a vacation. I was a chaperone on a mission trip to a Sioux reservation in North Dakota."

Adam shook his head. "Sounds like a vacation to me. I saw on the news that there was some pretty bad weather up that way. Did you get caught in a storm?"

"You might say that." She glanced at the open door, worried about James passing by the office on his nightly rounds. "I'd love to catch up, but let's get out of here first. I don't want to get caught sitting in front of the boss's computer."

Adam stood up. His eyes fixed on the shattered glass and the broken frame on the desk. "What happened? There's blood on Missy's folders, and you've destroyed the picture of her precious little darlings."

She shoved the frame and the tissues into her purse, grabbed the printout and shut down the computer. Adam stepped behind her, leaning in so closely that she could feel his warm breath on the back of her neck. A strange chill crept down her spine as she locked the door and returned the key to the secretary's drawer.

"You're a regular little Bond girl, aren't you? Should we add breaking and entering to your list of crimes?"

Adam's voice had a shrewd edge. It was almost as if he knew what had happened in Dagger Lake. But how was that possible?

It had taken her almost two years to get used to Adam's teasing, and then two more before she was able to see past it and count him as a friend.

During the day, the lab was illuminated by a row of overhead fluorescent bulbs that flooded the room with bright light. But after work hours, there were only a few low-wattage fixtures left on over the machines. Adam followed closely behind her as they walked toward her workstation, matching her pace as she slowed to skirt past the new shaker machine and stopping when she paused to straighten a tray of vials.

It felt like she was being tailed through the shadows by a stranger. She shook off that image as she reached up and turned on the small lamp on top of her desk. Maybe once she and Adam could see each other clearly, the strange sense of wariness she was feeling would disappear.

Adam seemed full of nervous energy as he leaned across her desk to straighten a pile of papers that had collapsed in a heap. "I'm dying to hear your big secret." He squinted at her through his tortoiseshell glasses and rubbed his goatee. "And please don't tell me you're looking for a new job. It would break my heart if I thought you came in to print your résumé when no one was around."

"Of course not! I love working here. And, if I ever did decide to leave, you'd be the first to know. Rest assured, I'm not going anywhere."

"I was just kidding. I know you live and die for Danford."

"Well, I wouldn't go that far, but you can trust me when I tell you I'm definitely not looking for another job."

"Good to hear." Adam ran the back of his hand across his forehead in a gesture of exaggerated relief. "So what are you doing skulking around like a thief in the night? Or am I going to have to torture the information out of you?"

"No torture necessary. I went into Missy's office to check the schedule for next week."

"So you stole the key and hacked into her computer?" Adam choked back an incredulous laugh. "You really must have been curious about your workload."

"It's a bit more complicated than that." Dani

bit the end of her fingernail as she considered the best place to begin. "I was in an accident in North Dakota. I never actually made it to the reservation."

"Wow." Adam's tone was flat.

"I know. And if getting stranded in a snow-storm wasn't enough, someone tried to kill me and set me up."

"What?" His eyes widened in surprise. "Why would anyone do that?"

"That's another really long story. But I think they hoped to keep me from returning home to testify."

Adam took a moment to consider this. "I'm not saying it makes any sense, but did you find anything on Missy's computer to support your theory?"

"Sort of," she said hedgingly. "I'm supposed to go to court on Tuesday in the Patrick Ravelli hit-and-run case. That was my only trial on the schedule."

"Patrick Ravelli? The state senator? Why would he want to set you up?"

Dani shrugged. "To discredit my reputation as an expert witness."

A thin scowl formed on Adam's face. "That seems unlikely. He's a millionaire who has a whole army of lawyers with nothing to do but defend his case."

"I know. But if they managed to paint me as unreliable, a jury might have a hard time believing my testimony about his DNA."

"Hmm." Adam resumed stroking his goatee. "I'm still not buying it. Why would a guy like Ravelli plant evidence in your van when there are hundreds of other ways to challenge a hostile witness?"

Warning bells sounded in Dani's brain. She had mentioned that she was being set up but hadn't revealed any details. There was no way Adam could have known something had been planted in her van.

A strange sort of excitement washed over her. Gideon was right. There was a connection between the cocaine and her testimony in the Ravelli case. But her giddy euphoria diminished as she realized that meant Adam was involved in the scheme.

But he was her friend. Surely, he would never deliberately do anything to hurt her.

"I really haven't been following the news," she said. Maybe if they talked long enough, she'd be able to figure out the extent of Adam's involvement. "I don't watch much TV or read the paper, so I'm out of the loop on the Ravelli case."

"Yeah, well, it's a big one." Adam leaned back against the worktable and smiled condescendingly. He began talking, but as she listened to the steady hum of his voice droning on about the evidence, her brain was working overtime to figure out how Adam fitted into the whole twisted scheme with the cocaine.

"The charges are based on circumstantial evidence," Adam insisted, continuing to lecture her about the details of the indictment. Even though she was only listening to every tenth word, she did manage to get the general gist of what he was saying. Apparently, he believed Ravelli had been unfairly charged by an overzealous prosecutor with an ax to grind.

"So, how did you get back to Iowa if your van was stuck in a ditch?" Adam leaned in toward her and caressed her hand. It was an effort not to recoil from his touch as she racked her brain to come up with an answer that didn't sound evasive.

"I got a ride with a friend I met at Dagger Lake." She regretted her words the moment they left her lips.

"Friend, huh?" His fingers stilled as they reached her elbow and then slowly crept forward, squeezing her upper arm. "Are we talking a boyfriend? Is he outside waiting for you in the car?"

She wished he was. A warm blush colored her cheeks. Gideon was most definitely not her boyfriend. He'd made it clear that his involvement extended only to clearing her name and protecting her from harm, and she felt an illogical desire to inform Adam of that. But she felt an even more desperate need to escape from his prying questions.

She twisted away from his touch and looked down at her hand. The pink stain of congealed blood from where she had cut herself on Missy's broken frame gave her an idea. She squeezed her wrist. Just as she hoped, the wound reopened and started to bleed.

"Will you excuse me a sec? I cut my hand in Missy's office, and I'd like to wash it off before I drip blood on my workstation."

Adam gave her a sly look. "I may have a Band-Aid in my desk drawer. Want me to check? I'd hate to wake up tomorrow and hear that you bled to death from a scratch on your wrist."

So much for that idea. She followed Adam to his workstation, where he pulled a package of Band-Aids from his desk drawer. Under normal circumstances she'd tease him about being overly prepared, but these were far from normal circumstances. Her pulse was thundering in her ears as she sorted through the package, searching for the right size bandage for her cut.

As she reached across the desk to hand him back the box, their eyes met, and she realized with a jolt of fear that he knew she was onto him.

But what drove an even deeper stake of panic through her heart was the knowledge that he seemed to enjoy watching her squirm. His eyes were cruel and mocking, and an amused smile twisted his lips.

"You always keep your work so neat and tidy." She was babbling, trying to act as if nothing was wrong, but the distraction didn't seem to be working. Adam adjusted his position to pin her against the wall. She edged closer to the side of his desk. If all else failed, she could vault over it and make a dash for the hall.

"I wish I had the energy to clean up after a long day." She mentally calculated the number of steps to the elevator. "But I'm usually in such a rush that I leave everything a mess."

"Not me." Adam's voice washed over her ears in a self-pleased purr. "I don't like to leave the building until everything is tidied up. I hate loose ends."

Was that a threat? She could feel fear rising in her throat, but she tried to stifle it. She had to remain calm and keep her thoughts clear until she made it out of the building.

"I wish I was like that," she agreed disingenuously. She glanced at his chair, where a navy hoodie was stretched along the back. Another chill ran down her spine as she remembered Josh and Gabe's description of the man in the church parking lot. If Adam had been the one to plant the drugs in the van, he was more involved in the scheme than she thought.

It felt like the walls of the office were closing in on her as Adam's face loomed closer and closer. She concentrated hard to keep her voice from shaking. "Thanks for the Band-Aid. Do you mind if I go to the ladies' room to clean my arm? I'll meet you back here when I'm done."

A flash of annoyance flickered in his eyes. "Sure thing, Dani. I'll just chill here, waiting for your return."

She had to force her legs to slow down as she stumbled toward the restroom door, ready for round number two of bathroom hide-and-seek. Back at the sheriff's office in Dagger Lake, she had been successful when she'd skipped out the back door of the station. Maybe she could try the same trick again.

Once inside the bathroom, she took a deep breath, her body shuddering as she leaned against the cool metal door. How could she escape with Adam just around the corner, watching and waiting for her to return? There was no solution except to take off running and hope to reach the elevator before he realized what was going on.

She took a deep breath and pushed open the door. The coast was clear. She began a brisk walk down the hall She could see the elevator. Only thirty more feet. She quickened her pace.

"Going somewhere?" Adam appeared out of nowhere, blocking her path.

She dropped her purse as she backed into a worktable behind her. A beaker toppled, shattering glass at her feet. Adam was closer. Much closer.

And he was holding her purse in his hand. "You didn't think I was going to let you get away that easily, did you?" He reached inside and pulled out the key card she needed to get out of the building. "And look what I found. It appears there will be no escape for you today."

Her brain scrambled to come up with a plan as she gripped the table behind her. She could feel her cut opening yet again as blood slowly started to trickle down her arm. With her left hand, she reached behind her, hoping to find something she could use against Adam.

Her fingers closed around a stapler.

Adam's eyes darkened as he lunged forward and grabbed her arm.

She twisted free from his grip and brought the stapler down on his head. He stumbled backward, a look of stunned surprise on his face as she took off running through the hall, down the stairs and into the second-level storage room.

* * *

A chilling gust whipped open the front of Gideon's jacket as he pedaled past the third blinking light in a row, his eyes scanning for vehicles in the cross street.

It had been at least five years since he'd ridden a bike, but it all came back in a flash. Well, at least the balancing part. He wasn't sure how long he could maintain his current speed on a ladies' bike with only three gears and a squishy tire. He had noticed the issue with the tire right away, but there was no time to stop and fill it with air. He needed to get to Danford, fast.

According to the map on his phone, the Port Reyes Office Park was a straight shot down Farrow Road. He just had to remember to turn left when he reached the last intersection.

The headlights of a vehicle behind him lit up the small mirror on the bike. He moved closer to the curb. But the semi flew past only inches from his lane, and he swerved out of the way. The sudden movement caused the front wheel to swivel sideways, tossing him headfirst into a ditch. He jumped back onto the bike and resumed his frantic pace. He was almost halfway to his destination, but his legs had started to shake from the pain. He was pushing himself harder than he ever had before, in a race against time, white knuckles against the handlebars, shoulders clenched against the cold.

Seven miles in, he was moving on sheer adrenaline. And horror at the memory of the voice of the man who had left the message on Dani's phone. Adam Zajac. "AZ," he had called himself with cloying familiarity. The guy sounded like someone who would eat kittens for breakfast. But Dani had said she considered him a friend.

He couldn't be certain, but an edge in AZ's voice set off alarm bells in his brain. Call it a gut reaction, but it seemed more than possible that Dani's friend Adam could be involved in the plot against her. It all made sense in a diabolical way. Of course, there was an inside connection at the lab. He should have realized it sooner and not wasted so much time focusing on Ravelli.

Thinking of Dani's kind face and sweet smile, he pumped the pedals harder, even as he clenched his muscles and his legs felt like heavy weights. He could no longer avoid the truth. He was in love with Dani Jones.

From the moment she had stepped out of the van in the snowstorm, he had known that there was something extraordinary about her. He'd watched her as she had interacted with the teens and noticed the gentle, caring way she dealt with each of them. He had studied her features as she bowed her head to say grace at his table and admired her firm resolve as she followed him through the tunnel and away from the fire. And even though she had initially been so afraid of Lou, that fear had quickly turned to affection. Who was he kidding? She had probably saved his dog's life.

Maybe she had saved Gideon's life, as well.

After thirty-five years, he had finally met the perfect woman, and because of his cynicism and lack of trust, he'd let her go.

But it wasn't over yet. Not by a long shot. He flew through three red lights as he approached the back entrance to the lab.

There was only one car in the front lot, a white Jeep with a Danford sticker inside the front window. It matched the description of the car Josh and Gabe had seen in the church lot, which meant there was a good chance Adam Zajac was still in the building.

Gideon moved toward the service entrance on the side of the lot. A jolt of relief throbbed through his senses. Someone had left the door propped open with a large stone. Maybe a security guard, tired of dealing with keys and locks on every building he had to check in the office park. At least now Gideon wouldn't need to break down a door.

He stepped inside a small hallway with the dark stairwell at the end.

It took less than a second to realize he'd made a mistake. Euphoria and exhaustion had caused him to forget his training.

A slight movement in the shadows caught his eye.

"Put your hands in the air and come out where I can see you," a gruff voice demanded.

EIGHTEEN

Gideon froze. Office security. In the space of three heartbeats, he considered his options and discarded all but one.

Dani needed him. Bottom line. End of story.

Turning slowly with his arms up, he made a pretense of surrendering.

"Hey, man. No problem here." He faced the officer, who appeared to be about fifty-five, out of shape and terrified. He stifled a groan. He hated using his combat training on one of the good guys. But he didn't have a choice.

In one swift maneuver, his left arm shot out and seized the officer's sleeve, while his right hand grabbed the officer's Taser. At the same moment, he thrust his booted foot and, in a clean sweep, kicked the officer's legs out from under him.

"I don't want to hurt you, but if you know what's good for you, don't follow me." He kicked away the rock propping open the service door and pushed the man into the lot. "Call 911," he shouted as the door slammed shut.

He was inside.

Or at least inside a dimly lit stairwell. Now all he had to do was find Dani before Adam Zajac did. He tried the door to the reception area, but it was locked. Apparently, a key card was needed to access the interior doors.

This place had tighter security than Langley. He charged up the stairs, taking them two at a time, and tried to open the door to the stairwell. Once again it was locked. Groaning with frustration, he punched the unyielding metal.

On the other side of the wall, he heard a scream and the clatter of something shattering against the ground. His heart pounding in his chest, he closed his eyes and before he even realized what he was doing, he began to pray.

"God, please let me save her. Please don't let my stubbornness and blindness cause another person to get hurt again." Then he added in a whisper, "I am so sorry. Sorry that I didn't seek You sooner. Sorry that I blamed You for all of the problems in my life. Please forgive me."

He had to get into the offices on the other side. The door was solid metal, so there was no possibility of breaking it down. He kicked the wall again in frustration, and his breath hitched when he noticed the dent left by his foot. The door might be solid, but the rest of the structure was nothing but drywall.

He punched the wall. Then punched it again and again until, fist bleeding, he broke through the surface in one solid crack. He began to tear down the plaster until he had a sizable hole. It was like peeling through the layers of an onion. Behind the drywall was a thick cardboard poster that appeared to be some sort of oversize advertisement for Danford Labs.

"'State-of-the-art techniques!'" He read aloud from the first sheet of paper he ripped from the wall. "'Advanced robotic technology!'" He yanked down that part down, too. Once he removed the posters, he ought to be on the other side.

But, of course, things were never that easy.

He found himself in a room surrounded on three sides by glass walls, with a door in the center that opened to the hall. He jiggled the handle, but it was locked from the outside. As far as he could see inside the space, there was no sign of Dani. But he knew she was in there somewhere.

He picked up one of the chairs at the long table and charged forward. Swung once, and then twice. The third time, the wall shattered. Finally, he was inside.

Dani slunk lower behind the tall metal shelf. From somewhere above her, she heard a crash and the sound of shattering glass, but she didn't dare make a move to investigate. After making her way down the interior stairwell to the second floor, she had barely enough time to find a hiding place before she heard Adam clunking down the stairs.

Oversize twenty-foot-high shelves lined the storage area in four long aisles. At-home DNA do-it-yourself kits, old equipment and out-of-date machinery competed for space and spilled into the corridors.

She inched forward on trembling knees, searching for a hiding place. She couldn't escape the building since she didn't have her key card. The stringent security at Danford Labs required employees to scan their ID badges not only upon entering but also upon exiting the building. But if she could just buy herself some time, James might appear on his rounds.

Her hand was still bleeding, and she had to stop every fifteen seconds to wipe away the crimson stain. Brushing her hair out of her face, she flattened her body against the nearest box as the door to the storage room swung open and shut with a clang.

"Daaaanniii," a voice called out. "Oh, Daaaannnii. Come out, come out, wherever you are."

"Please, God," she whispered. "Please don't let him come down this aisle first." She curled up in a tight ball and waited, her heartbeat drumming loudly in her ears.

A yellow beam of light swayed back and forth as it moved down the next aisle over. She estimated that she had forty-five seconds before Adam turned the corner and moved in her direction. It wasn't much, but it gave her some time.

Desperation made her frantic as she looked for a place to hide. Fear gripped her, but she refused to let it paralyze her. Any second now, Adam could lunge out and catch her.

"This is fun, isn't it?" Adam said. "I could have turned on the lights, but what can I say? I like a game of cat and mouse. Come out, little mouse. You know you can't escape. I know you can't escape. So why not entertain ourselves? At least for a little while. I do have for plans for today."

She inhaled sharply.

"Yes, my to-do list is full for the day. I need to do my grocery shopping and pick up a few Christmas gifts. Oh, and there is one more thing I'm forgetting. What could it be?" Adam had reached the end of the first aisle and rounded the corner. Just in time, she skirted around the last set of shelving, but not before she saw the metal gleam from the pistol in Adam's hand.

"Oh, that's right. Now I remember. I need to take care of one rather annoying loose end."

Loose end? That was her. The one person standing between Adam and a sizable payday. Her options were dwindling. She needed to find a better place to hide.

"You know, it didn't have to be like this." Adam was moving more slowly now, waving the flashlight up and down each shelf. "You were never supposed to be involved. But as always, you had to go and mess up my plans. Why did you have to arrive at work extra early the day the Ravelli sample arrived at the lab? It was supposed to be in my work queue. But little Miss Overachiever, I-Love-My-Job had to stick her nose out and dip into my business."

There was a loud clatter as a tray of test tubes hit the floor. "Guess you weren't hiding there. Why don't you just come out and the two of us can have a little talk? Not that either of us have all that much to say. To be honest, I'll be glad for the chance to eliminate you once and for all."

She shivered at his choice of words. There was no question that he intended to kill her. Catching sight of an empty cardboard box, she pulled it between two bins and slid inside, tugging the folds down above her. She huddled in the dark cramped space and fought the desire to cough.

She thought about Gideon and wondered if she would ever see him again. She wished she could tell him how sorry she was that she had sneaked out of the apartment without telling him. That she was so thankful for his help. That, despite the fear and terror of the past four days, she hadn't felt so safe with anyone since her sister's death. That, somehow, through all the tumult and excitement, she had fallen in love with him.

She thought about her neat stack of to-do lists and all her plans for the future. None of them mattered now. Sometime in the last fifteen years, she had allowed her coping mechanism to become an excuse. She'd filled her life with business, but keeping her mind occupied wasn't going to bring her sister back. And Ali wouldn't have wanted her to be alone.

The cardboard wall muffled Adam's rant but didn't smother out his words entirely.

"Do you have any idea what it was like for me?" His voice took on a petulant pitch. "Everybody said I didn't have the brains to excel at the job. And you?" His tone became laced with hate. "You were the worst. You never treated me like a man. Do you remember that I asked you out when we first started working together, four years ago? You were so offhand in your rejection that I knew you were just the same as everyone else. But I showed them. I'll show all of you. I'm nearly a millionaire now. I just wonder what would happen to our company's sterling reputation if I revealed how many DNA sam-

ples I corrupted or switched or destroyed over
the years. It's rather amusing when you consider
how Danford prides itself on its security, but it's
so easy to hack into Missy's computer.

"At first, I was just taking small bribes here
and there to provide negative paternity results
for men who didn't want to pay child support.
Nothing so grand. But then I corrupted my first
blood sample in a police investigation, and I
began to realize the power that came with the
job. Even that turned out to be small fry. But
once I learned that our lab was handling the Ravelli case, I knew it was the payday I had been
waiting for. Until you messed everything up by
taking over as the technician in charge."

Fear seeped into her bones as she heard a
click. A sliver of brightness appeared in the thin
crack in the box above her.

Adam had turned on the lights.

"Sorry to change the rules, but I was getting
bored of this game of hide-and-seek. I don't
know what your plan is, but you can't escape. It
is just you and me, sweetheart. Two overachiev-
ers stuck at the lab on a Sunday morning. Except
that I have a gun, and you don't. And my trigger
finger is starting to get itchy."

*Is this what Ali felt like when she realized es-
cape was no longer an option?* Dani wiped away
the silent tears flowing down her face and strug-

gled to control the all-encompassing terror as she waited for the inevitable. She could hear Adam's footsteps getting closer to her hiding place, so she closed her eyes and prayed.

Dear God. If I am going to die today, then that means I get to meet You and see Ali again, and that is a good thing. But please, please, Lord, don't allow my parents to grieve too much. And please don't let Gideon feel any guilt. He'll never know that I love him, so please pour forth Your grace and blessings upon him. I trust You, Jesus. I trust You.

A sense of calm settled over her just as a gunshot exploded through the air. Her heart leaped into her throat, and a scream escaped her lips.

"I told you my finger was itchy." Adam's voice sounded closer as his footsteps echoed against the concrete floor. Two more shots ricocheted off the wall. She covered her ears and huddled even lower in the box, reciting the Serenity Prayer over and over.

Adam fired again, and this time, his bullet hit its mark.

Pain sliced through her body. A circle of blood soaked through her shirt. She clutched herself and began to cough. More blood.

Pain dulled her senses as the box capsized, and her world tipped upside down. Flailing her arms, she tumbled out onto the floor as a shadow fell over her.

"Oh, there you are." Adam Zajac stared down at her, a bemused expression on his face.

If only she had the strength to grab something to throw at him. But her body was not cooperating. Her limbs were heavy as she curled up in the fetal position, clutching her abdomen.

Adam was talking, but he sounded so far away. Her body was shutting down as blackness settled around her.

"Goodbye, Dani," he said as a final shot tore through the air.

She tensed, expecting to feel the last bullet tear through her chest. But a second later, Adam fell down into his own pool of blood.

And then, out of nowhere, Gideon appeared. He knelt beside her, calling her name and tying something around her waist. His voice sounded hoarse as he shouted at her to stay with him. She wanted to tell him to stop, to just talk to her, but she didn't have the energy and the darkness was getting closer. She tried to smile at him before closing her eyes and letting go.

Gideon's brain had gone into autopilot, his hands robotically performing the emergency first aid he'd learned years earlier as a young recruit. Dani was losing blood fast. His hands moved feverishly, trying to make a tourniquet to slow the flow, but the wound was too deep. Her body was going into shock, and if help didn't arrive soon, he wasn't sure she'd make it. In the distance he could hear sirens wailing, and he pressed his hand to her bleeding abdomen, begging her to fight, to stay with him.

A minute later, the paramedics burst through the door and pushed him out of the way. And he sank to his knees.

NINETEEN

The nightmare rose like a foggy memory. She and Ali were running, faster and faster, but they couldn't escape. A sinister force moved closer and closer. A cry of fear bubbled up in her throat as she awoke in a room that was strangely familiar, like something she had seen on TV. Pale colored walls, a wide window looking out on a parking lot, metal bars on the side of her bed.

She was in the hospital. On cue, a red-haired nurse rushed into the room, carrying a plastic tote full of bottles and packets of gauze.

"Hey there, sleepyhead. We were wondering when you were going to open those pretty eyes of yours and say hello." The nurse was smiling as she pulled down the blanket to the end of the bed. "I'm just going to check your bandages. Your stitches seem to be healing nicely, but I need to take a peek at your tummy."

Dani's counselor had once told her that dreams had seasons, just like typhoons and hurricanes.

Dani was glad to be awake before another one rolled in and stirred up debris in the recesses of her mind. As she strained to adjust her position, a searing jolt of pain caused her to recoil from the caregiver's touch. The skin on her stomach was tight and burning, and for the first time, she noticed that she was hooked up to an IV.

"Your parents have been here all day, waiting for you to wake up," the nurse informed her. "They're going to be disappointed when they find out they missed the big moment. They just went downstairs to get some coffee, but I'm sure they'll be right back."

Hospital. Ambulance. The lab. Her mind flashed backwards through a series of fragmented memories. Adam pointing his gun at her with that maniacal grin on his face. A police siren wailing in the background, and Gideon kneeling beside her. Then strong, rough hands were loading her onto a gurney and into an ambulance. And then… The rest was a blur.

"How long have I been here?" She could barely recognize the feeble voice as her own.

The nurse checked her chart.

"You came in early yesterday morning and they took you into surgery right away. It took them a while to stitch you up and get your vitals back in line, but you came through like a champ. Your doctor will be stopping by in the next hour or so to see you. He'll be able to answer all your questions and explain about the operation."

Dani's cheeks grew warm. "The man who was with me? Is he okay?"

The nurse nodded. "I believed he was admitted and released within a few hours. He came to check on you, but you were in surgery. He stayed until they brought you back to ICU, and then he left."

"Has he been back since then?" Her voice trembled.

"I'm not sure. I got the impression he had business to take care of at home."

Dani turned to blink away tears. She needed to be happy. She was alive and soon she'd see her family. And Gideon was alive, too.

He had said from the outset that he didn't want to get emotionally involved, but it still hurt. The pain from the wound in her stomach was raw and searing, but it was nothing compared to the aching emptiness at the thought of Gideon driving away, job done, mission accomplished. Without even saying goodbye.

During the next few days, she began the long slow process of recovery. She was overjoyed to see her parents. The ordeal had taken its toll on them, and they were tearful and grateful that they hadn't lost her. The kids from her church youth group came by as well, the first time all together with flowers and candy and cards. After that, they had dropped by in twos and threes— Ellie, her most faithful visitor, had stopped in several times on her own to see how Dani was doing, with plenty of stories to share about the group's adventures at the reservation.

She felt better each day. Her stomach was still sensitive to the touch, but she could tell it was healing. Her heart, on the other hand, still ached with hurt. She thought a lot about Gideon, wondering why he hadn't stuck around to explain what had happened after she had been shot. And she thought about her future and how priorities needed to change. It was time to stop living for someone else.

At night, she slept. And dreamed. It was, after all, her season.

The glass doors of Miami International Airport swished open, and Gideon stepped out, rolling his sleeves as he headed for the nearest cab. The balmy seventy-degree weather felt almost tropical. He climbed into a taxi waiting at the curb and settled back in air-conditioned comfort for the thirty-minute ride across town.

He resisted the urge to call and check on Dani since he had spoken to her folks an hour before boarding his flight. According to her mom, she was still sleeping a lot, but the doctor had said it was normal after everything she had been through.

The muscles in his neck twitched with tension. Had he made the right decision? Would Dani understand that he needed to put his past behind him before he could even think about the future? Seeing her body crumple to the ground had caused a seismic reaction to his heart. At that moment, nothing mattered but becoming a man worthy enough to ask for her hand in marriage.

As the taxi passed a boulevard lined with palm trees, a flood of memories crowded his brain. Life had been good here. He had liked his job, his condo on the inlet and the camaraderie he shared with Jonas, his partner and best friend. Over the course of fifteen years, Jonas's family had become his family. Baptisms, weddings, funerals. He had been there for them all until the day of the shooting, when everyone was forced to choose sides. Why was he surprised that they had remained loyal to their kin?

The cabdriver pulled in front of a tall cement building in the heart of downtown. Gideon checked in at the front desk, made his way through two levels of security and took a seat in a stark waiting room on the third floor. Nervousness throbbed through his veins. He was about to face the man who had betrayed him, who had lied, stolen and killed for reasons Gideon still did not understand.

A buzzer pulsed, and a guard appeared with Prisoner 126 by his side. Two years behind bars had taken their toll on Jonas, and he looked a lot older than his thirty-five years. Though his light hair had been buzzed across his scalp, there were traces of gray at the temples and a few extra pounds on his usually lean frame. But even in an inmate's white jumpsuit, Gideon's ex-partner hadn't lost any of his swagger or shine.

Jonas met Gideon's eyes as he scraped a metal chair against the tile floor and took a seat at the table. "You lost your tan," he said, his lips curled up in an amused smile.

"It's winter in North Dakota."

"It's always summer in South Florida, man."

Silence filled the space between them. The guard shuffled his feet against the floor.

"I hear you filed for a new trial," Gideon said.

Jonas shrugged. "My lawyer thought it was worth a shot. I'm not a cold-blooded killer. I never meant to hurt the girl. You should know that. Remember all the times I risked my own life to avoid taking the kill shot? Sure, I set you up. But think about it. I had a wife and two kids. A family counting on me. You had no one."

Interesting logic. "You framed me because

you thought I had less to lose than you did," Gideon said.

"And lost my soul in the bargain." Jonas looked down and examined his fingernails. "You probably don't believe me, but if I had to do it all again, I'd play it straight. I did what I did in a moment of weakness. I needed money, and look where it got me? No one in my family wants to have anything to do with me. Not my wife. Not even my kids. Sure, they stood by me through the trial, but as soon as it was over, they turned heel and walked away. I write them letters, but they come back unopened and unread. You're the first visitor I've had in two months."

Gideon stared across the table at the man he'd once trusted with his life. Was Jonas telling the truth, or was it all just a ploy to gain his sympathies? It didn't matter. He hadn't come here to argue who had the better stake in the game. He had done enough of that in the past two years. This was about forgiveness and moving on. And becoming the man he wanted to be when he finally saw Dani at the hospital. After everything she had been through, she deserved only the best. It wouldn't do to offer her a heart still dark with anger and regret. What mattered was that he no longer felt that gnawing anger roiling in his gut. Gone was the all-consuming hatred.

In its place was a sense of peace and openness to forgive.

Jonas leaned forward and propped his chin on his hands. "You seem different. Changed. Back when we were partners, there was always a wariness about you, even when we were just kicking back with the guys. What happened, Marshall? Did that backwoods town of yours turn out to be more than just a place with a lot of snow and trees and open land?"

Should he tell Jonas about Dani? A small part of him wanted to keep his hopes and dreams a secret. But a bigger part wanted to shout it to the world.

"I met a woman," he said.

Jonas's face broke into a huge grin. "I'm glad for you, man. You deserve the best."

The guard jangled his keys, and Jonas pushed himself up with a reluctant smile. "So, that's it, then. You came, you saw, you did your thing."

Gideon shook his head. "We had a good run. And the way it ended doesn't change that. I'll never understand why you did what you did, but I've come to realize that it's not about understanding. It's about forgiveness. And I forgive you."

Ten minutes later, Gideon climbed back into a cab, his heart light. The anger that had been his constant companion for two years was gone.

In its place was peace. He hadn't come to see Jonas to make himself feel better about his life. He already felt pretty good about it. He was in love with an amazing woman. In the course of helping her, he had become reacquainted with a whole community of friends who had come through for him when he needed them. Through the grace of God, he had accomplished his mission. He had forgiven Jonas. It was time to go home.

The sound of footsteps woke Dani. She wondered if it was already morning, but when she looked around, the room was still cloaked in darkness.

She was surprised that Carla, the tall red-headed nurse who had been with her when she first came out of surgery, hadn't stopped in to say good-night at the end of her shift. Tonight, a new nurse had brought her meds and checked her vital signs. Carla, she explained, was spending Christmas Eve with her family.

Christmas Eve! When her parents left the hospital, they had mentioned something about attending midnight services, but the fact that it would soon be Christmas hadn't registered in her mind. She was still confused about the passage of time. In many ways, it seemed like ages ago that she and the kids had set off on their journey.

So much had happened in the past week, starting with that roller-coaster ride down the snowy embankment. There had been drugs and secret tunnels and icehouses. It made her sleepy just to think about it.

As she stirred into wakefulness, she felt strong, calloused fingers reaching for her hand, engulfing it with warmth and tenderness. The air was filled with the pungent smell of fresh pine. When she opened her eyes, a tall handsome stranger was sitting by her bed.

"Merry Christmas," he said.

She knew that voice. It had been echoing in her dreams for the last ten days.

Gideon.

He leaned forward, smiling. She hadn't recognized him at first. But the kind eyes she remembered so well were crinkling at the corners as they stared at her with worry and concern.

"You've shaved your beard," she said.

"I did." He ran a hand over his smooth jawline. "How are you feeling?"

"Pretty good. The doctors say I might be able to go home by the end of the week." She studied his face in amazement. Underneath all that hair was a fine, chiseled jaw and a face that was drop-dead gorgeous. Yet somehow she felt like she was looking at a stranger.

"That's great news." He tilted his head. "You

seem upset. Is everything okay? Do you want me to call the nurse?"

She looked away so that he wouldn't see her eyes filling up with tears. "I'm just wondering why you took off and didn't even tell me where you were going."

"Didn't you get the note I left with your things?"

She hadn't seen any note. She hadn't had the chance to look through any of the items in the clear plastic bag that the nurse had placed on the credenza after Dani had been moved from intensive care.

"It's been five days," she said.

"Oh, Dani." Gideon's face fell as he seemed to realize how much he had hurt her. "I thought you'd understand that it might take some time for me to sort this out."

"It's not like I've been pining away." She sniffled. "My parents have been to visit and so have the kids from the mission trip and my coworkers from Danford."

He seemed confused by her tone. "I'm glad you had company. And I'm sorry I couldn't get here sooner. Did anyone get you up to speed on what happened with the case?"

She shrugged. "They said they didn't want to upset me with the details."

"That makes sense. You've been through quite an ordeal."

They were both quiet for a few minutes, each of them waiting for the other one to speak.

"Is Adam okay?" She had to ask, though she wasn't completely sure how she felt about the answer.

"He is." Gideon seemed like he wanted to say something more but was making an effort to stop himself. "They patched him up, and the police took him into custody. Once they figured out what had happened, they got a warrant to search his place. They found records of all the tests he falsified the entire time he worked at Danford, as well as plenty of evidence to tie him to Ravelli."

"I've been so preoccupied. It never crossed my mind that I didn't show up to testify in the case. After everything that happened, it seems so unfair that Ravelli could go free."

"He didn't," Gideon said.

She noticed he was still holding her hand, but she didn't feel able to pull away. There was so much affection in his kind eyes that she almost forgot to feel upset that he hadn't called to see how she was doing.

"After the news broke about his attempt to tamper with evidence, Ravelli resigned from the legislature and pleaded guilty to the hit-and-run. He claimed he wasn't party to any of the extreme measures Zajac employed to interfere with his case. Ravelli did admit to contacting Zajac and paying him to alter the results. But once he handed over the cash, he thought that was the end of it. It might have been if not for the fact that you came in early and did the job Zajac had intended to do himself. That threw a monkey wrench into his plan. Zajac asked Ravelli for more money to eliminate you and discredit your reputation. And when Ravelli refused, Zajac resorted to blackmail. I suppose that was how he got the cash to buy the cocaine."

"So who were the men following me to Dagger Lake?"

"They were goons hired by Zajac to take you out and make sure that the drugs were found in your possession. It helped that one of the deputies at the sheriff's office was on his payroll."

"So Adam was the mastermind of the whole scheme?" She was having trouble wrapping her head around the fact that a man she had known for years had hated her that much.

"That's what it looks like at this point. I'm sure he'll do his best to implicate Ravelli when the case goes to trial, but with all the evidence against him, it might be hard to convince a jury that he is an innocent pawn in someone else's game."

She settled back against the pillows on her bed. For the first time, she looked past Gideon toward the corner of her hospital room where a small pine strung with tiny white lights was set on a table by the wall.

"It's a Christmas tree," she said.

"I cut it early this morning before I set out on the drive. Your nurse told me it was against hospital rules, but she said she'd make a special exception for her sweetest patient."

She took a deep breath. She sure didn't feel all that sweet at the moment. She actually felt rather irritable.

"Thank you for going to all that trouble, Gideon. But I'm still confused about why you came back here after all this time. I had just about given up on ever seeing you again. I thought you were still mad that I sneaked off and ended up facing down Adam on my own."

"You didn't know what you were up against. Adam Zajac had everyone fooled, not just you. If I was mad at anyone, it was at myself for not realizing there had to be a connection to someone at the lab."

She bit her lip and looked away. Somehow that didn't make her feel any better.

"I always planned to come back to see you, Dani. You need to believe me. When you got shot, I went crazy. My brain went on automatic shutdown once they loaded you into that ambulance and took you away. When I got to the hospital, I couldn't even breathe until I was sure you were okay."

"When you left, I was still unconscious." Try as she might, she couldn't disguise the cold and the hurt in her voice.

"I didn't want to go. I wanted to wait until you woke up. But the doctor said it might take a while for your body to recover from the trauma you sustained. I was trying to decide what to do when I saw your parents arrive at the ICU. After everything they had been through already, it seemed right to allow them some time alone with you. Besides, I thought it might be awkward for them to see some guy with blood-stained clothing and an unkempt beard hanging around by your bedside. I wanted to meet them under better circumstances. And today, I did."

"What?" With all the surprising things he had just told her, that had to be the most shocking. "You met my folks? When? Why?"

"Just a few hours ago. I stopped by their house before I came to see you. After I got back to Dagger Lake, I called to let them know what had happened at the lab and how brave you had been throughout the whole ordeal. I've actually been talking to your mom on the phone every day to keep tabs on your recovery."

"You called my parents? I wonder why they didn't mention it."

"Probably because I asked them not to. There were a number of issues I needed to work out that were just too complicated to explain. But I wanted them to know what we had been through together and to explain why I couldn't stay. I needed to return Pete's car and talk to Cal about the situation in Iowa. That whole mess took way too long to sort out. But you have to believe that I was doing everything in my power to make it back as soon as I could."

He paused. "There was something else, too, a personal issue I needed to work through. For the last two years, I've been determined not to allow anyone to get close enough to hurt me. I shut out my friends, my community. God. I was angry. Angry and alone. I needed time to sort out my soul. Before I could even think of offering you my heart, I had to make sure all the bitterness was gone. So, three days ago, I went to Miami to visit my old partner in prison."

"Prison?"

"It's a long story, but seeing Jonas again allowed me to let go of all the hatred and to forgive. I got back yesterday. And then I had to stop at Abby's to pick something up."

She wondered what he needed to get from Abby, but even as she asked herself the question, she knew. The look on Gideon's face gave it away. He was staring at her with eyes so full of love that it couldn't be anything else.

"I wanted to ask her for our mom's engagement ring so I could give it to you." He smiled, and her eyes filled with happy tears. "Dani, when I saw you bleeding on the storage room floor, I realized what it would feel like to lose you, and I didn't like it at all. I know I've been stubborn and obstinate. You have seen me at my worst. But in that moment, I prayed that God would give me the chance to ask for your forgiveness and let me tell you how dearly I love you with all of my heart. And I promised that, no matter what happened, I was turning my life over to Him."

"Oh, Gideon," she said. "You saved my life. And I've spent all this time imagining the worst. I thought you had gone back to Dagger Lake, angry at me for getting you involved in an impossible situation. You paid a huge price for doing a good deed and taking all of us into your cabin. Lou got stabbed and your barn burned down and… Oh," she said, remembering something important that she needed to ask before he said anything else. "Is Lou okay?"

"He's fine. He's hobbling around with a big ole cast on his leg, but Abby said that it's not keeping him from getting into trouble. But we need to get back to business before your nurse comes in and kicks me out. It's Christmas, after all, and I think there's a package for you under the tree."

He stood and walked over to the pine in the corner, then picked up the maroon velvet box underneath. Reaching inside, he took out a ring and knelt in front of her bed.

"Danika Jones, will you do me the great honor of agreeing to be my wife? If you can look past all my faults and transgressions and say yes, you'll make me the happiest man in the world."

"Yes, Gideon. I love you so dearly, and it will be my greatest joy to marry you." Her eyes filled with tears as she stared into the face of the man she loved. Gideon. Her protector through the storm.

EPILOGUE

Five months later...

It was quiet enough to hear a pin drop in the courtroom.

"On count one," the foreman said, "we, the jury, find the defendant, Adam Zajac, guilty of attempted murder."

Dani closed her eyes as a whirlwind of emotions collided in her head. Relief. Gratitude. And sadness for the man who had once been her friend. She listened as the remaining charges were read. Aggravated assault. Evidence tampering. Conspiracy to transport drugs across state lines. All rendered the same response from the foreman. Guilty on all charges. There would be a sentencing hearing in a few weeks, and after that, Adam would be remanded to the state penitentiary, where, according to mandated guidelines, he would begin serving a minimum of ten years.

The verdict itself came as no surprise. During the week-long trial, the district attorney had painted a picture of a man corrupted by money and prestige, a man for whom blackmail and murder were the inevitable results of a dangerous game. There was no shortage of witnesses to attest to the scope of Adam's misdeeds, most important Gideon and Dani, whose testimony made it difficult, if not impossible, for the defense attorney to challenge the facts.

Chairs scraped across the floor as the judge and jury exited the courtroom. Dani opened her eyes, dismayed to discover that her fingernails were digging hard into Gideon's palm.

"Sorry," she said. "I'm still shocked that Adam will be going to jail."

"He tried to kill you, Dani," Gideon growled. "And look at the problems he caused for Danford. It's going to take years for them to regain the public's trust. The only bright spot is that you'll be there, making sure the tests are done right and the proper protocols are followed with every sample of DNA."

Dani felt a rush of pleasure at his response. It hadn't been easy, but she and Gideon had reached a decision about where they would live when they were married. Gideon would relocate to Blooming Prairie, and she would continue working at the lab. At least for the immediate future. But she'd cut back on her hours and start living in the present instead of viewing her work as a legacy to the past.

She turned to her mother and father, sitting on the other side of her, and offered them a smile. She was glad she and Gideon would be living near her parents for the time being. But once they started a family, they planned to return to Dagger Lake. She hoped to persuade her mom and dad to make the move, as well.

Dani swiveled back to her husband-to-be. "Now that the trial is over, I can focus on our wedding. It's hard to believe it's less than a month away. There are so many things on my to-do list that I hardly know where to start."

"Your list?" Gideon raised a brow in pretend consternation. "How about all the stuff I need to do?"

"True," Dani conceded. Gideon did have quite a few loose ends to tie up before starting a new job as consultant to the local police. At least he wouldn't need to pack up all his furniture and gear since they planned to keep the cabin and maintain his ties to the tribe and the Dagger Lake community.

At the top of both their lists was house hunting for a place with a yard big enough for Lou to have plenty of room to play. The move would be tough on him, as well. He had gotten used to more relaxed country ways.

The next few weeks were bound to be busy. Despite a pledge to keep things simple, the guest list for the wedding continued to expand. With all of the late RSVPs, the VFW hall in Dagger Lake would be packed to the rafters with relatives and friends.

If only Ali could be there, as well.

Dani reached up and touched the medallion she still wore around her neck. Serenity, courage and wisdom. It had been her prayer in the past, and it would continue to be in the future as she embarked on a new life with Gideon, her most cherished true love.

* * * * *

If you enjoyed this book, pick up these other exciting stories from Love Inspired Suspense:

Battle Tested *by Laura Scott*
Undercover Memories *by Lenora Worth*
Amish Christmas Secrets *by Debby Giusti*
In Too Deep *by Sharon Dunn*
Grave Peril *by Mary Alford*

*Find more great reads at
www.LoveInspired.com.*

Dear Reader,

It was 1985 when forensic scientists first tapped into the evidence encoded in our genes—DNA. Unique as fingerprints, samples of blood, hair, bone and tissue discovered at a crime scene could be analyzed, and a match to a likely suspect could be made. Over the past thirty years, DNA testing has become standard procedure in cases like the one involving Dani's sister. It was this evidence that enabled police to find her murderer and bring closure to her grieving family. No wonder Dani dedicated her life to unlocking the mysteries of DNA.

Although I am not a scientist, I have always been fascinated by DNA. How incredible to consider these intricate details of God's creation, which were once hidden and are now evident for all to see. We have only to look to Genesis 4:10 to find a hint about the information God has concealed in our genes. "And He said, 'What hast thou done? the voice of thy brother's blood crieth unto me from the ground.'"

Thank you for joining Gideon and Dani on their winter adventure. I'd be honored to hear

from you. You can email me at JayceeABull-
ard@gmail.com, or friend me at Facebook.com/
Jaycee.Bullard.1.

Warm regards,
Jaycee Bullard

Get 4 FREE REWARDS!

We'll send you 2 FREE Books <u>plus</u> 2 FREE Mystery Gifts.

Harlequin® Heartwarming™ Larger-Print books feature traditional values of home, family, community and most of all—love.

FREE
Value Over
$20

YES! Please send me 2 FREE Harlequin® Heartwarming™ Larger-Print novels and my 2 FREE mystery gifts (gifts worth about $10 retail). After receiving them, if I don't wish to receive any more books, I can return the shipping statement marked "cancel." If I don't cancel, I will receive 4 brand-new larger-print novels every month and be billed just $5.49 per book in the U.S. or $6.24 per book in Canada. That's a savings of at least 19% off the cover price. It's quite a bargain! Shipping and handling is just 50¢ per book in the U.S. and 75¢ per book in Canada*. I understand that accepting the 2 free books and gifts places me under no obligation to buy anything. I can always return a shipment and cancel at any time. The free books and gifts are mine to keep no matter what I decide.

161/361 IDN GMY3

Name (please print)

Address   Apt. #

City   State/Province   Zip/Postal Code

Mail to the **Reader Service:**
IN U.S.A.: P.O. Box 1341, Buffalo, NY 14240-8531
IN CANADA: P.O. Box 603, Fort Erie, Ontario L2A 5X3

Want to try two free books from another series! Call 1-800-873-8635 or visit www.ReaderService.com.

---

*Terms and prices subject to change without notice. Prices do not include applicable taxes. Sales tax applicable in N.Y. Canadian residents will be charged applicable taxes. Offer not valid in Quebec. This offer is limited to one order per household. Books received may not be as shown. Not valid for current subscribers to Harlequin Heartwarming Larger-Print books. All orders subject to approval. Credit or debit balances in a customer's account(s) may be offset by any other outstanding balance owed by or to the customer. Please allow 4 to 6 weeks for delivery. Offer available while quantities last.

Your Privacy—The Reader Service is committed to protecting your privacy. Our Privacy Policy is available online at www.ReaderService.com or upon request from the Reader Service. We make a portion of our mailing list available to reputable third parties that offer products we believe may interest you. If you prefer that we not exchange your name with third parties, or if you wish to clarify or modify your communication preferences, please visit us at www.ReaderService.com/consumerschoice or write to us at Reader Service Preference Service, P.O. Box 9062, Buffalo, NY 14240-9062. Include your complete name and address.

HW18

HOME on the RANCH

YES! Please send me the **Home on the Ranch Collection** in Larger Print. This collection begins with 3 FREE books and 2 FREE gifts in the first shipment. Along with my 3 free books, I'll also get the next 4 books from the Home on the Ranch Collection, in LARGER PRINT, which I may either return and owe nothing, or keep for the low price of $5.24 U.S./ $5.89 CDN each plus $2.99 for shipping and handling per shipment*. If I decide to continue, about once a month for 8 months I will get 6 or 7 more books, but will only need to pay for 4. That means 2 or 3 books in every shipment will be FREE! If I decide to keep the entire collection, I'll have paid for only 32 books because 19 books are FREE! I understand that accepting the 3 free books and gifts places me under no obligation to buy anything. I can always return a shipment and cancel at any time. My free books and gifts are mine to keep no matter what I decide.

268 HCN 3760 468 HCN 3760

Name   (PLEASE PRINT)

Address   Apt. #

City   State/Prov.   Zip/Postal Code

Signature (if under 18, a parent or guardian must sign)

Mail to the **Reader Service:**

IN U.S.A.: P.O. Box 1341, Buffalo, New York 14240-8531
IN CANADA: P.O. Box 603, Fort Erie, Ontario L2A 5X3

HRCBPA18R